BENDER'S L.A.

ALSO BY MICHAEL ELIAS

Novels
Night Dive
You Can Go Home Now
The Last Conquistador

Screenplays
The Jerk (with Steve Martin and Carl Gottlieb)
The Frisco Kid
Young Doctors in Love
Lush Life
Serial
Trick Baby
Envoyer Les Violons
No Laughing Matter
A Dead Man in Deptford

Selected Television
Head of the Class
All in the Family
The Dick Van Dyke Show
The Odd Couple
The Mary Tyler Moore Show

Praise for *Bender's L.A.*

"In the last few years, Michael Elias has become one of my favorite writers. And *Bender's L.A.* is, as far as I'm concerned, the best work he has ever done. I was in heaven reading it."
—Lili Anolik, author of *Didon and Babitz*

"Michael Elias writes with humor and precision. The sentences flow easily and inevitably along. I loved this book."
—Steve Martin

"Elias mixes Bender's politics as he experiences Hollywood in a tumultuous decade of war and revolution, with his hero's constant self-reflection and analysis. And that Hollywood is never far from any moment internal or external in Bender's life makes it all even more interesting — doubles it up, folds it over — as every story is a story and yet could also be a story about a story about a story. I love it all."
—Jessica Anya Blau, author of *Mary Jane*

"It's a great read — an elegy for lost loves and lost cities, and a love letter to L.A. Cynical, social satire and emotional truth. Eve Babitz meets Raymond Chandler."
—Patrick McGilligan, author of *Young Orson*

"There is a seductive matter-of-fact quality to this novel that combines with a liquid clarity. With these people there is no doubt you know your onions.
—Phillip Davison, author of *The Crooked Man*

"This has the wry humor of Scott Fitzgerald's Pat Hobby stories, refracted through the cracked lens of *L.A. Confidential*. Sublime."
—John Baxter, author of *A Year in Paris*

BENDER'S L.A.

Michael Elias

Sticking Place Books
New York

Sticking Place Books 2026
stickingplacebooks.com

Cover illustration © Deborah Blum
Designed by Michael Zikovitz, Freewheel Design

ISBN 979-8-89976-068-6

Nothing is funnier than unhappiness.

Samuel Beckett, *Endgame*

For Eve Babitz

Of our disastrous trip to Palm Springs in
Slow Days, Fast Company you wrote:
"Since both David and you promised to supply me with
your own personal versions of this adventure,
I've been expecting at least something.
But neither of you has come up with a single morsel."

I'm sorry it took so long, but here is *Bender's L.A.*
I'm in yours as David, you're in mine as Mimi.

WE/T HOLLYWOOD

Bender sulked in the hot tub, his dog asleep on a foam pad, its tail thwacking in a mutt dream, nose twitching for the scent of a coyote looking for a fight or a waiting raccoon savoring its own dip in the steaming water should Bender, depressingly high on a smoked-down joint, leave and neglect to cover the wooden tub. Bender reflected, as he often did, on the time in Puerto Vallarta when Ellen said she no longer wanted to be married to him.

"Why?"

"Because we'd be better off."

He heard a wave crash. Then another.

"Why?"

"Because we came to Hollywood," Ellen said. "Because I am unhappy here. I miss New York, I don't like show business, or your Hollywood friends and their shitty politics. They only hate the Vietnam War because their kids might get drafted. I'm lost in a place I can't leave."

"But you can leave me?"

"It would be a start, Bender."

"Why?"

"It's the way you look at women at the next table. It's that thing you do with your olives, the way you dunk and nibble them, and the fact that you treat me like a wife."

"But you are my wife."

"That's what I mean."

"But why did we come fifteen hundred miles to Mexico to tell me you want a divorce?"

"And also, the whys. Mexico was a test. You knew we were on shaky ground. You shouldn't have agreed to come. That's another thing I can't stand. Your cowardice. You're always giving in to me. I need someone stronger."

"What if we hadn't come to LA?"

"That's another thing. All the what ifs?"

Bender took a breath and dunked into the steaming water where he counted what ifs? What if they had stayed in Manhattan? What if Bender had landed a writing job on *Saturday Night Live*, what if Ellen had gone to law school after Hunter, been hired by the ACLU, it would have all added up to a move to the Upper West Side, shopping at Gristedes, a summer rental in the Hamptons, skating at Rockefeller Center, enrolling their street-smart children in private schools, and then what? Would their marriage be intact instead of fucked up on a white beach in Mexico.

In New York, Bender submitted jokes and sketches to comedians and agents, earning money as a substitute teacher in the public schools; he was a jack of all trades, adept at math, science, art, Spanish, facing rooms of surly adolescents ready to do combat with the 'sub.' He measured teaching days like a fur trapper counting pelts: four pelts paid the rent at their apartment on the Lower East Side; three bought groceries for a month, two got them movies, an off-Broadway play and dinner in Chinatown. Ellen worked weekend nights at Joe Allen and fed Bender when she was on duty. They weren't poor, they weren't rich, they were two American immigrants in Manhattan, learning the language of the city, finding their burrows and nests in the Village, then Soho, finally settling on 12th Street in the East Village, priced out of the world of Capote and Mailer, they didn't care, or even notice, they *got by*, they were their own first loves. Their apartment had a gas refrigerator, barred windows overlooking a field of junk, and no sink in the bathroom, but Allen Ginsberg lived upstairs. They never ate in a restaurant that owned a *La* or *Les*, but alternated between Ratner's and Max's, with an occasional stop at the B.& H., or a fat eggroll at the entrance to the IRT on Astor Place.

Finally, Dick Colby at William Morris passed Bender's material on to Ernie Chambers, a television producer in Los Angeles, who offered him a job with a one-way plane ticket. Bender and Ellen rented a small house in Beverly Glen. Ellen enrolled in UCLA law school, he reported to work as a junior writer on a doomed variety show, the last of its genre, hosted by a fading Mouseketeer. By the end of the run Bender saw the future: adapt or die. He learned to write sitcoms, became a client of Neil Navitz, who was on his way to becoming the most powerful agent in Hollywood. Now Bender counted sitcom episodes as pelts; three were a down payment on a house in Benedict Canyon, two bought season seats to the Lakers, one provided a month of psychoanalysis with Dr. Grotstein in Westwood, residuals paid for Ellen's law school. To what end? Bender was a working writer with a promising career in Hollywood, but he missed *getting by* in New York, artist's loft parties in the Bowery with Ellen, Sundays in Washington Square, chess and folksingers, Judson Poets, The Living Theatre, and La Mama. There were no eggrolls on the way to the subway, there were no subways. Bender drove numbered freeways to work, divorced from his wife and his past.

Bender dipped the stub of the joint in the tub and tossed it into a stand of mottled opuntia cacti. Smoking weed didn't help; it only intensified his misery over a gone wife. Under the influence Bender created green-eyed scenarios and conversations, he wrote them in his mind, he pictured Ellen with powerful attorneys, their romantic dinners, road trips in better cars than his, their giddy endless sex. Bender confessed his fantasies in twice-weekly sessions to Dr. Grotstein from his leather couch, sought advice from friends, strangers in bars. He cast the question in Platonic terms: *Was divorce, as Socrates asked Meno regarding virtue, learned or acquired?* In his own family there was only one; distant cousins he barely knew. His parents gossiped about it in Yiddish to keep it from the children, but secretary and motel had no equivalent in the language of shtetl Jews, the words crept into their conversation, so eventually he learned infidelity was the issue.

Bender's Puerto Vallarta memories refused to retreat. He had run into the Pacific Ocean, battled weak waves, swam a hundred yards, and returned to the *sombrillo*, hoping to hear Ellen say, "Just kidding, Bender. I wouldn't divorce you for all the guacamole in Mexico." But Ellen was gone. There was a note under the Dos Equis bottle: 'I'm going back to L.A. I'll be at Maria's. You can stay in the house. We'll talk in a few days.'

Like other misguided couples uncoupling, they hired lawyers who maneuvered them into arguments, followed by depositions, suits and countersuits until they were legally divorced and broke. But as that was the future, this was the present, as much as Bender ached, as much as Bender wept, as much as Bender wanted Ellen back in his bed, or to be in hers, he also wanted an answer.

Why?

But then, so did Ellen: when Bender told Ellen he loved her she replied, "Why?"

Bender said because: *You have a nose that is almost perfect but perfect because it isn't, a face for Botticelli to paint, a smile to disarm Nixon, you are beyond sexy,* and it was true, but they were male reasons and Ellen tossed them in the feminist wastebasket. Bender said because: *You are erudite, creative, speak French, and possess a fine sense of humor,* it was true, but Ellen only shrugged. Bender said because: *You are an astute Marxist, anti-Stalinist, respected by Tom Hayden, familiar with Akhmatova, you quote Brecht, you will be an important lawyer and keep Angela Davis out of jail.* Ellen shook her head.

Bender said because: *You are Stones over Beatles, Country Joe over Joan Baez.* Ellen said she had changed her mind and now preferred Joan.

Bender said: *If you were not in my life, I would not be who I am, I would be no one.*

"But I would," Ellen said.

Bender ignored the cruelty, reread the Sonnets, consulted Browning, Virgil, Marlowe, Snoopy, Hallmark; he plagiarized, borrowed, rephrased, but if there was a reason that satisfied Ellen's *why,* he couldn't find it. Bender took his case to Dr. Grotstein who suggested she might feel unworthy of love and not accept Bender's reasons for loving her, nor anyone else's, until she was able to love herself. "And, that Mr. Bender, is her problem, not yours."

Bender said, "Maybe I don't love her. Or, worse, what if I love her because she doesn't love me."

"That," Dr. Grotstein said, "is a candidate for examination." And then, in a detour from their rigorous Freudian analysis, Dr. Grotstein added, "Do you know the story about the man who goes to a voodoo priestess?"

"No."

"The man says, 'My wife has left me. I'm brokenhearted. Can you help me?' 'Yes, my darling. I can make your wife be in love with you, or I can make you forget her. Which do you prefer?'"

"I see what you mean," Bender said.

There was a silence. Dr. Grotstein announced their time was over. In the elevator, Bender knew the choice was obvious. The problem was where to find a voodoo priestess.

o   o   o

Bender hoisted himself out of the tub, the cold night air erasing memories of Ellen and Mexico. He fitted the wooden cover over the water, dressed, put his dog in a cage to prevent it from chewing furniture, got into his 1954 Alfa Romeo Giulietta, a car of such temperamental nature that when Bender turned the key in the ignition, he had already done something wrong. Fortunately, from his house in Benedict Canyon it was downhill to Sunset, and if necessary, Bender could coast to Santa Monica Boulevard and walk to Dan Tana's restaurant. As he drove, Bender wondered if Ellen would have been happier if he owned a new Mercedes, joined Hillcrest, played golf, drank at the Chateau Marmont bar instead of Ports, a quirky restaurant at the dark end of Hollywood where Jacques, the owner, handed his keys to the last customer and told him or her to lock up. Would Ellen still be his wife?

Not likely. She drove a Honda, hated country clubs, was deep into the anti-Vietnam War movement, radical feminism, and had abandoned the literary evenings at Ports to Bender as she spent her time at Weather Underground coffee shops in Venice and East L.A.

On K-EARTH, Neil Diamond was begging Sweet Caroline to return. Did a song ever bring a woman back? What if Sweet Caroline heard the song and knocked on Neil's door? Would Neil send his present wife packing?

Not likely.

Should Bender write a come-back-to-me song? Would Ellen be his wife again if he did?

Not likely.

Bender's Alfa brought him to Dan Tana's without incident. A red-checkered tablecloth restaurant, its two dining rooms divided by a bar, Dan Tana's clientele included old and new Hollywood, actors, indie filmmakers, artists, racetrack bettors flush with cash on their way to Santa Anita or broke on their way back. Mirroring Los Angeles geography, the booths on the west side were more desirable; studio executives, producers and stars got the best ones. The eastern side was reserved for tourists.

Bender found a stool at the bar, waved to a *Tonight Show* writer sipping Coke with lemon, a sure sign of an AA member. Like a misplaced movie camera, the horizontal mirror behind the rows of bottles projected bisected torsos of waiters carrying plates of food to diners. Bender stared upward at his reflection, bowed his head to see if his round bald spot was still there (it was). He considered his face; it evoked his father's Hungary, his mother's Russia; a prominent nose, (father) defined cheekbones and chin (mother), brown eyes and brown hair that still had traces of its youthful red. If Bender stood up, he would be over six feet, but he possessed a gentle manner, a desire to please, genuine modesty, he never intimidated. Bender knew he wasn't classically handsome, but he could pass for a character actor, the leading man's best friend. In Hollywood, beauty can also be a disadvantage, less for men as it is for women; if you are too good looking you must be dumb. One night, at Tana's bar a woman thought Bender was a famous actor.

"I'm not."

"You look like one."

"Who?" Bender asked.

"Dustin Hoffman."

"I'm taller but thank you."

Bender waved at the television producer who hired him over dessert, "You eat faster than me, Bender, you'll take short lunches." And the time he arrived late; Ellen was already at the bar. "Some jerk's been hitting on me. I told him I was waiting for my husband, but he wouldn't give up."

"I'll take care of it. Where is this asshole?"

"He went to the bathroom. I watched him go; he hit on two other women on the way there." She looked up at the mirror. "Here he comes."

Wilt Chamberlin squeezed into a space next to Bender.

"So? Are you going to say something?" Ellen whispered, her tongue licking his ear. There was a *why*, something he loved about her. Had he complimented her tongue?

Bender remembered the night he saw Lew Wasserman and Henry Kissinger squeeze through the crowd on their way to the prized corner booth. Henry Kissinger, murderer of Vietnamese, Chileans, Bangladeshis, bomber of Cambodia. The list of his crimes was longer than Wasserman's movies. Bender reached for his gun, an easy shot, if he had one; karate would do. He would spare Wasserman, but not Kissinger. Bender downed his drink, imagined himself sliding off the bar stool, following Kissinger to the tiny bathroom standing at the lone urinal, pissing an old man's piss; feeling his bladder's need to vacate, waiting patiently for the message to travel to his brain and order the liquid to flow.

"This is for Salvador Allende," Bender said.

"What?"

A *shuto-uchi* to the throat. Kissinger dropped to his knees.

"And the thirty thousand disappeared in Chile." Another strike to the back of the neck. "For Cambodia."

A man hobbled out of the toilet stall, his pants around his ankles. A witness to Bender's revenge. "Nice work, brother."

"Thanks."

Bender stepped over Kissinger's limp body.

At the bar Ellen said, "Did you do it?"

"Yes."

"You're my hero, Bender. Mexico was a mistake, I was wrong. Take me home."

Bender nibbled his olives, ordered another martini, and tried to figure out why he couldn't imagine freedom from Ellen as easily as killing Henry Kissinger.

Bender felt a shoulder tap. It was Mimi Betz, a writer who was finishing her first novel. Bender had read parts of it with envy. If Mimi could stay safe and sober, she would be an L.A. literary giantess. She was witty, fearless, and despite one foggy semester at City College she had outread any male Ivy ranger in range. Mimi was also Hollywood High beautiful; she smiled white Chiclet teeth, shook real blonde hair, had a chorus girl figure; her past lovers included a movie star, a comedy star, a rock and roll star, a MoMA curator, and her present lover, Paul, an up-and-coming art star, whose first show at Molly Barnes sold out before it opened.

Mimi gave Bender a quick cheek kiss. Bender offered Mimi a sip of his martini.

"No way. I've got sixty days."

"Fantastic."

Mimi meant AA meetings at Rodeo, Robertson, Pico, dots on the Los Angeles map for recovery, alcohol, cocaine, and pills. In her tenuous early days Bender drove Mimi to meetings where people he knew welcomed him: "Bender, I'm so happy to see you here. Let me know if you need a sponsor." Bender said he was there for Mimi; he didn't have a drinking problem. He got sympathetic nods, found a seat, listened to "personal stories" at once heartbreaking and funny. He witnessed cakes presented to members for their days or years of sobriety. Bender was skeptical of its success, averse to prayer, and left meetings with a sore throat from the cigarette smoke. Sobriety at the expense of emphysema. He took to waiting in the car for Mimi.

"And say hello to Anthony," Mimi said. A slim serious man with a wispy mustache and octagonal eyeglasses, Anthony shook hands with Bender while he scanned the room, shaking his head in disapproval. Bender figured he was counting phonies and sell-outs.

Bender whispered to Mimi, "Do I know this guy?"

"He writes about politics for *The New Yorker*."

The maître d' waved; they followed him to a table. A busboy brought menus, a basket of bread, filled their water glasses. Tana's food was borderless Italian; dishes were named for celebrities, all friends of the owner. Bender had once ordered a complete named dinner: *Chopped Salad à la*

Nicky Hilton, Veal Rollatini Mo Rothman, Potatoes Beckerman, ending with *Tiramisu Nadia Comaneci.*

Paul scanned the room for celebrities. "There's Roy Scheider."

"He's facing the wall, doesn't want to be noticed," said Mimi. "You see Michael Landon over there, in the booth, back to the wall, as in *please notice me.*"

"Oh, man, is that Sterling Hayden?" asked Paul. "He's one of my favorite actors."

"Christ, don't stare," Anthony said.

"He's a movie star. He's at a middle table, it means he wants you to stare," Paul said.

"He's alone. Let's ask him to join us," Mimi said.

"We should respect his privacy," Anthony said.

"Fuck that," Mimi said. "Order me a George Hamilton, medium rare." She walked to Hayden's table and began chatting. A few minutes later, Hayden stood up, put some cash on top of his check, and lumbered over to their table with Mimi. Bender made room for Hayden; he was a big man, six-five, still gloriously fit and handsome.

A Hollywood native, Mimi was an expert in handling movie stars, able to walk a conversational line between breathless idolatry and sincere admiration, smart enough to flatter but not fawn, praising performances in movies that weren't big hits. As they ate their celebrity-named dishes, Hayden sipped his scotch, speaking in his trademark rapid-fire diction, ending sentences with *huh, hum, don't you know.* He was sizing them up, deciding whether they were worth any more time than a couple of drinks before he went back to his hotel. When the waiter brought the check, Hayden reached for it. "The studio is paying," he said.

They thanked him profusely.

Hayden said, "Well, since you are such pleasant company, intelligent and literate, why don't you come back to my hotel where we'll continue our conversation in the comfort of my suite. We'll drink, smoke and be merry."

Mimi pinched Bender under the table.

At the curb valet station, Bender, not wanting to take any chances with his Alfa Romeo proposed they ride in Paul's Toyota. Hayden climbed in the front seat with Paul. Mimi, Bender and Anthony squeezed into the rear.

"I'm at the Century Plaza. Do you know it?" Hayden said.

"Sure. Used to be the Fox lot, you made a lot of pictures there," Paul said.

"I did. And if you think this will be an evening of gossip and motion picture stories, I assure you it will not. Hum? We will be discussing politics, art, and literature. I want argument, I want strong opinions held and defended. Do we all agree? Hum?"

It was not the first time Bender had heard that admonition. At certain Brentwood dinner parties, hosts forbade conversation about movies or television. Bender figured it was probably the same in Detroit, where you weren't allowed to discuss brakes or horsepower.

Anthony's voice came out of the darkness: "Mr. Hayden, I was at the Union Square anti-Vietnam War demonstration. You made a great speech."

"You were there?"

"Yes, sir, I was. I will never forget it."

"Well, that was an important moment, don't you know. I was doing a picture for Irv Kershner. I said, 'Irv, I'm going to be sick Friday so you may want to adjust the schedule.' Kersh said, 'Me too. See you there. It's in the budget as a location scouting trip to Union Square.' Kersh was a good no-nonsense guy. Why the hell he ended up doing one of those sci-fi crapos I don't know. Actually, I do. He needed the money. Who's got some Mary Jane?"

Paul produced two freshly rolled joints, which were lit and passed. The Toyota was filled with sweet smoke. Mimi, staying sober, lolled her head out of the open window.

At the Century Plaza, Paul was reluctant to turn over his car, reeking of marijuana, to the parking attendants. The valet captain was insulted at the implication that one of his drivers might damage the vehicle. He could understand this reluctance from a Ferrari or Rolls owner but not from the driver of a piece of shit Toyota. Bender obtained a pledge that the car's odor would not be reported to the police and added a five-dollar bill. In the elevator Hayden hummed a tune, towering over everyone. He turned to Mimi. "We are only five. When we get to my room, I want you to round up a few more like-minded friends. I hate small groups. But no agents or producers. Hum?"

Mimi said, "I'll call Warren and Tanya, they'll come over in a minute."

Bender considered a call to Ellen. Would she enjoy meeting Sterling Hayden, impressed that her ex-husband was hanging out with a movie star? Probably not.

"Tell them to bring their own Mary Jane," Hayden said.

"Sure," Mimi said. The 'sure' took Bender out of his fantasy and reminded him what he liked about Mimi. When a current lover slept with another woman or returned to a wife, Mimi drove to Benedict Canyon and crawled into bed with Bender. "We can't have sex, but I'd like to cry on your shoulder. I know it's a cliché, but I also like you."

"It's okay. I like you, too."

"Even though you were a jerk in Palm Springs."

"I was in a cast from my ankle to my balls, and Ellen wouldn't answer my calls."

"She also threw a tire iron at you in the parking lot and said she was angry that she had spent all those dreary years married to a male chauvinist pig."

"Did she? Why don't I remember that part?"

Mimi laughed and kissed him. Since they were in bed, it made sense to ignore the commandment that friends should never be lovers. Afterwards Mimi said, "You're not over your ex-wife. I would be crazy to be in a relationship with you. You'd dump me in a minute if she came back to you."

Bender returned a diplomatic shrug, knowing if Ellen called to reconcile it would be less than a minute.

At the hotel door, Hayden asked everyone to repeat their names. When it was Bender's turn, Hayden said, "Do you have a first name, lad?"

"David. But everyone calls me Bender."

"I changed mine to John Hamilton when I joined the Marines. I didn't want to be Sterling Hayden actor slash movie star. No special treatment. When people would ask me if I was Sterling Hayden, I said I was his double. Of course, they found out, but by then I was assigned to the OSS and parachuting into Yugoslavia to fight with Tito's partisans. I was just Big John to them. I won a Silver Star for bravery and was personally decorated by Tito." Bender was happy to be in the hallway of the Century Plaza Hotel next to this movie star, a war hero, a writer, adventurer, someone who clearly fit Aristotle's *megalopsuchos*, a great-souled man. Bender was falling in love, which is what movie stars make you do. He wasn't thinking about impressing Ellen, unravelling why she had left him or who was kissing her now.

Hayden unlocked the door, shooed everyone in. "Make yourselves comfortable, but don't touch anything. I want a word with this lad." He shut the door, put his hands on Bender's shoulders and pulled him close. Bender wondered if Hayden was going to kiss him.

"It means a lot to me that you were at Union Square, that you heard my speech. I'm proud of that day."

Bender considered telling Hayden it was Anthony at Union Square, but only for a moment.

"I'll never forget your speech," Bender said. "It was a significant moment in my life."

Hayden looked deep into Bender's eyes. "We will be friends, lad. You can count on that, hum?"

"That's great, Mr. Hayden."

"Call me Big John."

"Yes, Big John."

o   o   o

Hayden's suite overlooked the 20th Century Fox backlot; the view stretched from Beverly Hills to the Pacific. He had transformed the living room from a sterile corporate hotel space into his own with Moroccan fabrics draped over the furniture, framed Picasso and Matisse reproductions, nautical maps and family pictures covering the walls. A Bang & Olufsen audio system rested on the desk, next to a La Pavoni espresso machine. Art books, a bowl of seashells, a sextant, a globe sat on the coffee table. A brass antique telescope on a tripod was aimed west to Brentwood.

Mimi hung up the phone. "They're on their way."

"It's an amazing room, Mr. Hayden," Paul said.

"I travel with three sea trunks. It's the only way to live in a hotel, don't you know? That's my chair, sit anywhere else. Mimi, please call room service and tell them Big John wants food and drink for seven. They know what to do." He sat down, kicked off his shoes, stretched out his long legs. "I went through the war. I jumped out of bombers, yet, when I get a close-up in front of a camera I curl up and die. Each man to his own fears, um? Toss me one of those cigars, will you, Bender, help yourself. Cuban, don't you know, I can't say how I get them. I started at the top and worked my way down. I don't think there are many other professions where you can be paid good money and not know what you are doing."

"Maybe you just can't watch yourself on screen," Mimi said.

"No maybes about it. If I had the dough, I'd buy up the negative of every film I was in and start one hell of a fire, hum? I say an actor is only a pawn, don't you know, brilliant sometimes, rare, and talented, capable of bringing pleasure and even inspiration but if you asked Brando, he'd say the same thing. We're just pawns. Highly paid pawns. I did nothing in '57 and Paramount still paid me $70,000."

Bender had heard the "highly paid" speech before from actors who had lived through the Depression and could never reconcile making so much money for such easy work. Hayden rose out of his chair, went to the telescope.

"I set this up so I could look at the boats in the bay and my old homes. The one on Tigertail Road, you can't see it now, the trees are too high, but I found the one in Santa Monica."

He swung the telescope around. "Come here, everybody. Line up for a look at Big John's favorite beach house. Only a nickel."

When it was Mimi's turn, she said, "I know that house. Eddie Blum lived there."

"That's right. I bought it from him. He was a good man, excellent writer, wrote *Stalag 17*. Wouldn't join the Party. I can't blame him. You probably know I was a Communist. A lousy one, I'll be the first to admit, but in Yugoslavia when the going got rough and it was time to be counted, it was the Reds who stood up and fought the Nazis. I'm probably the only man who bought a yacht and joined the Communist Party on the same day."

Warren and Tanya stood up. "It's been a pleasure, Mr. Hayden, but we have to go," Warren said.

"Why?"

"It's almost morning."

"Nonsense. It'll be daybreak soon. We'll drive to the beach swim. Steak and eggs at Patrick's and then we can all go to work. Sit down." Warren and Tanya returned to the couch.

"Mimi, honey, since you're the only one sober, I want you to read something if you don't mind. Right there next to you is a copy of my book, *Exiled*. Turn to page two hundred and thirty-eight and you will see the appropriate section. It's underlined."

Mimi opened the book, flipped through the pages.

"Out loud."

"Sure." Mimi adjusted a lamp, read:

We are ruled not by patriotism but by greed. Success is measured by fat wallets while others starve. We toil at meaningless jobs; we buy what we don't need and end up in debt for it. We give up our childhood innocence for adult cynicism. Our children follow us, and it becomes a vicious cycle. Who will reject this path? Who will take the road that leads away from the poverty of the wallet and to the richness of the soul?

"Profound," Paul said.

Hayden stood up. "Damn right it is. Okay, everyone go home. I have an early call. Except you, Bender. I want a further word."

As his guests filed out Hayden shook hands with the men and kissed the women on both cheeks. To Mimi, he said, "You read me beautifully, my dear."

When they were alone, Hayden said, "Light us up a farewell doobie, lad."

"I'm out, Big John."

"In the teak cigarette box on the TV."

Bender opened the box. Inside there were a dozen neatly rolled marijuana cigarettes. Hayden selected one, lit it with a worn brass Zippo engraved with a US Marine Corps emblem. He took two deep hits, handed it to Bender.

"You have any idea why I asked you to stay, lad?"

"I don't."

"Because you were in Union Square. You heard my speech on the war. You were a witness to the one moment in my life of which I am justifiably proud."

"As you have every right to be. I told you that."

"When I was younger, I was a member of the Communist Party, don't you know."

"You mentioned it, sir."

"Stop calling me 'sir.' I was subpoenaed before the House Un-American Activities Committee. I cooperated. I was a friendly witness. Which is a polite way of saying I was a one-shot stoolie show. A real daddy-long-legs of a worm when it came to crawling. I ratted out my friends. The people I named were blacklisted and deprived of their livelihood." Hayden leaned forward, grabbed Bender's shoulders, shook him like a palm frond. "I'm a bastard, Bender. I'm scum. You understand?" Hayden's face came in and out of focus, his voice alternating between a booming echo, then a squeaky soprano.

"Something funny, lad?"

"What am I smoking, Big John?"

"Humboldt mixed with Turkish hash. My private blend."

"I'm fucked up, Big John," Bender said.

"Nonsense. You only had two puffs. Have another."

"No thanks, Big John. Your turn."

Hayden took a massive inhale, the end of the joint glowed like a traffic light. "I respect you, Bender. You were there. You heard me speak at Union Square. Your opinion counts."

Tell him.

"My opinion?"

Tell him.

"Lad, I'm talking to you." It was the stern voice of Hayden the sea captain.

Bender stood up. He didn't float to the ceiling. He was strangely sober, out of excuses. "I wasn't there."

"What?"

"It wasn't me. At Union Square. It was Anthony. He was the one who heard your speech. Not me."

"You lied?"

"I'm sorry, Big John."

"Well, I guess neither of us has clean hands, hum?" Hayden squeezed the roach into a ball and swallowed it. "Why?"

"I think I wanted to make a good impression," Bender said.

"I know that instinct. It didn't work out that well for me, or the people I ratted out."

"Big John, listen to me, you're different from the others; the ones who testified and named names."

"How so?"

"You're sorry for what you did, you apologized, that's a big deal. People respect you. You're not like the others. You're a good guy."

"That's nice to hear, kid, but I'm still a lousy worm."

"Not to me, Big John."

Hayden narrowed his eyes, "For sure?"

"For sure."

"I can call my Teamster. Drive you home."

"I'm okay. I'll walk back to Tana's. I need the air."

Hayden opened the door. "Elevators to the left."

"There's more to my story, Big John. It's also about betrayal. Can I tell you?" Bender said.

"I don't have time to hear it, son."

"One day, then. It was nice meeting you."

"You, too, Bender. Come and visit me in Paris. My barge is just west of the Pont Alexandre III. It's the one with a green roof."

Bender stepped out of the lobby of the Century Plaza Hotel. It was early morning in Los Angeles, but agents were already taking breakfast meetings with studio executives, actors who were working that day were finishing make-up and hair, calls were being placed to New York, where it was almost ten o'clock. Bender saw Henry Kissinger get out of a limousine. The attack would be easy; pretend to be an old friend, handshake un-refused, followed by a bear hug. He knew a pressure point to bring Kissinger's murdering heart to a dead stop. But Bender was tired. Better to kill him another time.

On his walk to Tana's, Bender remembered when he and Ellen went to Paris. On the plane they each chose a Paris writer and created a walking tour of their haunts. Bender picked Henry Miller, looked forward to the Café Wepler "the epicenter of sex," and Rue de la Gaité, with its former brothels and bars; Ellen went first and named Simone de Beauvoir, Bender cowardly followed with Gertrude Stein. As a result, they were subjected to Simone's surly waiters with a table next to the bathroom steps at the Café de Flore, and a grim tour of Sorbonne hallways; as for Gertrude, she rarely left her house on the Rue de Fleurus, preferring Alice and her own salon. If they got back together, Bender would take Ellen to Paris to meet his pal, Sterling Hayden, and stay on his barge on the Seine. He would take them to the Flore and get a good table.

Dan Tana's was closed, the parking lot empty except for his Alfa Romeo. There was a note on the windshield, *keys on left tire.*

That afternoon, Bender's agent, Neal Navitz called. "I heard you left Tana's with Sterling Hayden."

"We hung out with him at the Century Plaza."

"Did you pitch anything?"

"No, we just hung out."

"Time well spent," Navitz said. "I want my writers to know film actors. Alex Roberts likes your screenplay. He has some notes; he wants you to come to Aspen. Shouldn't be more than a week. Paramount will get you a condo. You'll love Alex. He's a genius."

A/PEN

A week later Bender was sharing a taxi to Aspen with Melinda Dworkin, the woman he met in the boarding area of United Airlines who said she liked his socks. From there it was a loose and easy conversation, on the plane a generous passenger switched seats with him so he could sit next to Melinda. By the time they landed in Aspen, David Bender of Benedict Canyon, and Melinda Dworkin of somewhere in Chicago were scheduled for dinner after his meeting with the genius director. Bender weighed the pros and cons of Melinda: she didn't look him directly in the eye, she had a nervous giggle between sentences that was just short of annoying. On the other hand, she was interestingly pretty, well-read, he liked her smile; if Bender was sensitive, behaved like a perfect gentleman, things might work out.

The studio provided the genius director with a Richard Meier house in Woody Creek. The all-white building disappeared in the winter, in the summer, it was an eyesore to the neighbors. It had a pool, tennis court, ski hut, a Porsche, and a new Ford Bronco in the driveway. Bender compared it to his condo and made a note to be a director in his next life.

"Get settled, dude," the genius director said after a welcome coffee, "We'll start fresh tomorrow. I have some family stuff tonight anyway. So tell me more about your dinner date. How did you guys meet?"

"Pure coincidence."

"What the fuck does that mean?"

Bender knew this was a man who didn't like coincidences on screen and off. "I'm not sure. We just started talking while we were waiting for the plane."

"You're the dog. I gotta tell you I'm envious."

A five-million-dollar director envious? Of what? His ability to meet an interesting woman? In Hollywood, envy was first cousin to schadenfreude. If the genius director was envious, then Bender's downfall would be his pleasure. Best to be careful.

"Good looking?"

"Okay."

"Great body?"

"Hard to tell."

"Cool. Well, have fun tonight. We'll start at ten tomorrow, okay?"

o   o   o

Bender knew the Hotel Jerome when it had a funky cowboy ambience. Funky was now starting at $500 a night. Melinda Dworkin must also be a woman of means. He called her from the lobby.

"Hello, Bender. Can I take you to dinner?" Melinda said.

"I was about to say the same."

"I went first. Please?"

"Okay."

"Oh, thank you. I'll be right down."

In the restaurant Melinda ordered a bottle of Veuve Clicquot.

Bender began: "I was going out with a lot of women, and getting involved, but I was still in love with my ex-wife. I couldn't commit, but I wouldn't admit it. The more miserable I was, the harder I fell for women. The truth is I wasn't fit for human consumption. My shrink said I was trying to solve depression with distraction, but I realized as a way of life it was pathetic." Bender didn't mention that he was also having a lot of sex, so it wasn't that pathetic.

"Did you break many hearts?" Melinda asked.

"A few."

"And now?"

Bender recalled Dr. Thom Marshalik's workshops at Esalen he had taken to get over his heartbreak: *Connecting Through Conflict and Letting Go, Moving On*. Marshalik had two mantras: "Hold on, stand still. Let go, move on." There was another, but Bender couldn't remember it. "I'm okay, really."

In an unusual spasm of responsible behavior, Bender decided not to try to get this woman to fall for him, or he for her, as he hadn't *let go*, he hadn't *moved on*. He would not tell Melinda his funny stories, be charming, compliment her, quote Sylvia Plath, or eat lightly, but it didn't make any difference. As she was paying the check, Melinda said, "Will you come up to my room?"

"Yes."

"Thank you."

Thank you?

Did Melinda shut her eyes as they made love? The room was too dark to tell. Afterward, Bender smoked a cigarette on the balcony. Under the full moon, the snowless ski trails were wide vertical lawns. The night air carried Mahler from the Aspen Music Festival to Melinda's room. She switched on the bedside light. Melinda sat against the velvet headboard, the sheets bunched around her torso, like an actress who refuses to do nude scenes.

"Would you drop the sheets so I can see how lovely you are?" Bender said.

Melinda did. Bender saw whom he had touched and felt. Black hair over ivory white skin, slightly uneven breasts, a tiny stomach roll and a delicious scrape on her knee that hadn't quite healed. She wore a thin gold chain with a cylindrical Mezuzah.

"Bender?" Melinda said.

"Yes?"

"Come sit."

"The cigarette."

He was naked, he couldn't stamp it out. Should he toss it over the balcony on a passing Music Festival cellist?

"Bring it with you. I want a puff."

She made room on the bed. Bender handed Melinda the cigarette.

"I think it's two hundred dollars if they smell tobacco," he said.

"I can afford it."

"Are you rich in Chicago, Melinda?"

"Sort of. Are you in Hollywood?"

"I'm okay. I can afford anything except blue chip art."

"How do you live in Hollywood? Isn't it superficial?"

"Where life is possible, then it is possible to live the right life; life is possible in Hollywood, so it is possible to live the right life in Hollywood."

"Oh, Bender, you're a Stoic. How sweet."

This wasn't going well. Melinda knew the *Meditations of Marcus Aurelius*, ordered champagne in French, her body was perfect in its imperfections, and she was from Chicago, a city of writers, the home of Nelson Algren, Langston Hughes, Clancy Sigal, Carl Sandburg. Find flaws, Bender thought, find flaws, you must not fall in love with this woman, or she with you. You are still obsessed with your ex-wife, you ache and plot for her return, this will not end well, you will hurt Melinda From Chicago. Bender put forth his best anti-falling-in-love challenge, guaranteed to anger a still warm bedmate: "Do you mind if I watch the second half of the Lakers game? They're playing the Bulls."

"Oh, my God! I'm a major Bulls fan. I'll order some popcorn."

The next day, Bender sensed grumpiness in the genius director. "I want to get rid of the flashbacks."

"I'm open to that. Sometimes you can explain too much. I trust your judgement."

The director's mood improved. "So how was your date last night?"

"What can I say? She's a big fan of your work."

"That's nice to know. Did you consummate?"

Consummate? Where was this guy coming from, Havelock Ellis?

Still wary, Bender said, "Frankly, I don't think it's going to happen. No chemistry if you know what I mean."

"It's all chemistry, man."

"Hey, I forgot to tell you, I met your ex. Ellen, right? She's a terrific lady."

Blood doesn't boil, Bender thought. It's just a dumb expression. Don't ask him the how, why, or when he met Ellen. Change the subject. He heard Dr. Marshalik, "Move on, Bender."

"So how'd you guys meet?" Bender asked.

"Dinner with Dan Melnick. I think they're dating. He's reading one of your screenplays. About an art heist. He likes it. Navitz sent it to me, too, but it's not for me."

Bender was losing count of his boiling blood bubbles: Ellen, Melnick, the genius director, Navitz.

"Wait, am I picking up some pain? You still pining? Oh, man, tell me you guys are cool, right?"

"We're cool. We're friends."

"I know how it is. My first wife and I split up, the whole year I was a paranoid, hostile, drunk jerk, it's a wonder I'm still in the business. And you know what?"

"What?"

"The whole time I thought I was a perfect gentleman."

"How'd you get over it?"

"Three w's: work, weed, women."

Bender thought for a moment. "You ever try voodoo?"

"Seriously?"

"Yes."

"I wish I had known."

Bender was beginning to like the genius director. Joints were offered, but Bender declined, then relented, an hour later they were mildly stoned, but still able to work.

"Let's look at the discovery scene."

The genius director read the scene aloud, then lectured Bender as if he was a first-year film student: "The audience needs to know exactly how the ransom money ended up in the Dean's office. You haven't written a credible reason, Bender. I need one. The audience needs one."

Bender knew the story of Bob Garland, hired to do a draft of *The Electric Horseman.* He was never able to satisfy Sydney Pollack how Jane Fonda finds Robert Redford in the Nevada desert. Garland tried everything from bloodhounds to flyovers in helicopters. Pollack rejected all his ideas, fired him, and found another writer. When Garland saw the film, the solution was revealed:

Redford: "How did you find me?"

Fonda: "It was on the map."

"Bender? Are you with me?"

"Yes, yes. I agree. It's something we need to solve. I promise, I'll find a way."

They spent the rest of the session making cuts to the screenplay, changing nights to days to save money as they came down from their high.

"Do you have any plans this evening?" the director said.

"I have a hot date with our script."

"What about your girlfriend?"

Bender shrugged. The less this genius knew the better. "She's going to the Music Festival. You?"

"Dinner with an agent trying to poach me. He's flying in."

"Pages tonight or tomorrow first thing?"

"Tomorrow. But can we start in the late afternoon? We're going mountain biking in the morning."

"Sure."

"Do you ride?"

Bender knew a non-invitation when he heard one. "Not since junior high school."

Walking to his condo, Bender was serenaded by barking dogs tied to the beds of pick-up trucks.

o   o   o

In his room Bender called Melinda. "I have some work tonight. Are you up for a late dinner?"

"Do you cook, Bender?"

"I do, but…"

"I'll bring food. Nine o'clock?"

"Sure."

"Thank you."

The screenplay rewrite went smoothly. The director's suggestions made sense; all Bender had to do was make sure the story stayed coherent. Changing nights to days was more complicated but he moved one scene indoors, finessed the others. How the ransom money got into the Dean's office would come to him eventually so for now, fuck it. Bender was finished by eight, he had an hour to kill. He took a long shower, dipped in and out of some television, set the table, turned on the radio and settled into an Adirondack chair on the balcony to wait for a Rocky Mountain sunset and the arrival of Ms. Dworkin From Chicago. Both events accompanied by 'All John Denver All the Time' on the radio. As he hoisted himself out of his chair to change the station, the phone rang in the bedroom.

John Denver nasaled on, "*You fill up my senses like a night in a forest.*"

"Bender?"

"Ellen?"

"Where are you?"

"I'm in Aspen. Paramount sent me here to work on my script with Alex Roberts. He said he met you."

"Little guy, thinks he's a genius?"

"Yes."

Ellen laughed. "A dope. You're the genius."

That was strange, Bender thought. Had she just complimented him? "Is something wrong?"

"I'm fine. You called me, I'm returning your call," Ellen said.

This was even stranger. She rarely returned his calls. When they first split up Bender invented excuses to telephone, once he said, "Do you have my copy of *Midnight's Children*? And maybe we should try couples therapy."

Just before she hung up, Ellen said, "Couples therapy is for couples. We're not a couple."

"What's up, Ellen?"

"I've been thinking. Maybe we should see each other when you get back from Aspen."

Bender reached over and changed the station. Ray Davies was singing "Waterloo Sunset." "As in talk?"

"Yes."

"What happened to Melnick? Alex Roberts said you guys were dating."

"We're not, I saw him a few times."

"I hear he's a nice guy," Bender said, a weak attempt to move on.

"It's a long story. He wasn't a nice guy, okay. It turned out he was a jerk. When do you get back to L.A.?"

The doorbell rang. "Just a minute."

Ms. Dworkin, smiling, held up a large shopping bag. "Chinese."

"I'm just finishing this call," Bender said.

"Take your time, I'll unpack."

Bender took the phone into the bedroom. Melinda was singing along with Ray:

Every day I look at the world from my window

Sha-la-la

Bender took a deep breath; "Ellen, Dr. Marshalik said I have to move on."

"Seriously? For the last year you've been telling me you still love me, you can't live without me, we need to be together, and now suddenly you want to move on? Bender, you're pathetic."

Ellen hung up.

Bender went into the kitchen. "That was my ex-wife." He was telling Melinda the truth. Where would this end?

But I don't feel afraid

As long as I gaze on Waterloo sunset, I am in paradise.

"She's having a hard time," Bender said.

"Just be nice to her."

"I will."

What had he done? Ellen just told him she was having second thoughts, and he had told her he wanted to move on. Bender remembered a Carol Burnett sketch he wrote for Harvey Korman and Tim Conway that satirized quiz shows. Harvey, playing the host, gives contestant Tim a choice between two boxes, he chooses one, opens it, reaches in, and takes out a feather.

Harvey says, "A feather! Well, that's disappointing! Shall we see what's in the other box?" He reaches in, retrieves a single key. "Why this is just a key. What door does it open? Shall we see?" A curtain opens revealing a brand-new Cadillac convertible, in the back seat there is a bag of golf clubs, a television set, and a set of luggage.

"That's right, if you had picked the other box, the key to this Cadillac and the fabulous gifts, plus $10,000 cash in the glove compartment — would all be yours! But good luck and thanks for coming on the show."

Tim says, "I want to go again."

Bender said, "I want to go again."

"What?" Melinda said.

"Would you excuse me for a minute?"

"Sure."

Bender went back into the bedroom, dialed, and got Ellen's voicemail:

"Hi, this is Ellen. Leave a message and I'll call you back. If this is you know who, drop dead."

He returned to the kitchen; Melinda handed him a plate. "You're not over her."

"No."

"Time, Bender. Time. You'll see."

o   o   o

Bender made tea; they ate Chinese food and had two interesting conversations. One about intervention in foreign conflicts, the other about conceptual art. Melinda was against intervention, he hated conceptual art. Bender thought if Melinda could figure out how the ransom money got in the Dean's office, he would have to propose marriage on the spot. He tried to find something he didn't like about Melinda, he couldn't, but there was one little rat in his brain gnawing away. He couldn't see the rat yet, but he knew it was there. Was it *thank you* after sex?

On Sunday, Bender borrowed the director's Porsche and drove Melinda to the airport. They were early. They walked to the edge of the runway and watched the planes take off.

"Can you fly, Bender?"

"I once took glider lessons," Bender said.

"That sounds like fun."

"Up to a point. I was on the verge of getting my license; the last requirement was a solo flight. Then I realized I shouldn't do things where I will die if I make a mistake, so I quit. I also don't sky dive, rock climb, or write a producer's life stories."

"Are you a coward, Bender?"

"I wrestle with it. Can I visit you in Chicago? Or can you come to Los Angeles?"

"You've been wonderful. But I don't think so."

As stories went, it was pretty good. Bender debated telling it to the genius director who had called to cancel Monday's work session.

"I fell off my bike coming down Spar Gulch," the director said. "I didn't feel anything at first, but when we got to the base of the mountain the guys in the bike shack had to turn a hose on me to wash off the blood. Did you ever see a William Morris agent faint? In the winter you ski on those trails, and you forget when the snow melts the little rocks are as sharp as diamonds. I need you to stay a few more days. I'm still kind of fucked up on codeine. What's the latest with your girlfriend?"

"She went back to Chicago."

"You going to see her again?"

Bender shrugged. "Different lives, you know how it is."

"Tell me about it."

Bender knew the director only meant this as an expression of agreement, but he told him anyway.

o   o   o

"I was a junior at Northwestern, living at home," Melinda said. "One day I couldn't leave my room. I just couldn't. I watched TV, read, even moved a piano into my bedroom, but I was afraid to leave. It was too terrifying. I had serious agoraphobia."

"Don't they have meds now?"

"I tried them. Didn't work. My mother found a psychiatrist who made house calls. It took him a year to get me out of my bedroom, but I still couldn't leave the house."

"How did he do it?"

"Talk therapy plus assignments."

"Like?"

"Walk to the front door. When I was able to do that, then I had to walk to the front door and touch the doorknob."

Bender was way ahead of Melinda, but he let her tell it.

"Eventually, he got me out of the house," she said.

"Do you have a job?"

"My father owns an art gallery. I sit in the back, do inventory."

"Do you still see the shrink?"

"Yes."

"He continues to give you assignments?"

"Yes."

"Name one."

"I had to go to a karaoke bar. And sing."

"Another."

"I had to start a fight with my father. Then quit. Then find a new job."

"Another."

"Pick a place I've never been, fly there by myself a few times."

"You chose Aspen."

"Yes."

"How many times?"

"Three."

"And then?"

"I had to meet a man, spend the weekend with him."

"And sleep with him?"

"No. That was my decision."

"Why Aspen?"

"John Denver, I guess. I love John Denver."

o   o   o

"You're fucking kidding me," the director said.

"It's true. I swear."

"Is there a movie in it?"

"I could make the shrink crazy. He's training her to kill somebody. We could call it *The Fatal Assignment*," Bender said.

"I like it. Who do you see?"

"Goldie Hawn."

"I hear she's looking for something dark."

There was more but Bender didn't tell him.

o   o   o

At the curb Bender handed Melinda her suitcase. "Do you feel used, Bender?" she said.

"Yes."

"I'm sorry."

"It's okay. Used is also being useful," Bender said stoically.

"I am getting better. You helped. Thank you."

"Why don't you ask your shrink to assign you to come to Hollywood?"

"I don't know. That sounds scary."

"Is your real name Melinda Dworkin?"

She kissed him. "No, but I know yours."

o   o   o

At his condo, Bender checked his voicemail. There was no message from Ellen. But one from Navitz: "Good news. I set up a meeting with Marty Ransohoff. He wants to be in the Bender business. Marty's a major force in television; he wants you to write a pilot."

Bender thought about calling Ellen to give her this good news, but there was no point, she wasn't returning his calls. Bender had no one to whom he could give good news.

HOLMBY HILLS

Bender drove his Alfa Romeo down Benedict Canyon, made a right onto Sunset Boulevard, past Ladera Drive, he turned right again on Carolwood Drive for his 8 a.m. meeting with Marty Ransohoff. In the morning Marty offered a sliding menu: bagels and cream cheese for sitcom writers, screenwriters were given smoked salmon with their bagels; studio executives, A-list stars and directors were served Eggs Benedict. After the meeting, Marty drove to his office suite at Columbia. Furnished in French Provincial, the walls covered with posters of Marty's films and Impressionist oils on the walls. Cary Grant once said, "Marty's Monets are fake but they're the best in Hollywood." Marty ate lunch at his own table in the executive dining room, and hosted elegant dinner parties at his home, prepared by a live-in French chef who had cooked at The George V.

Marty was considered a tough guy. Bender also knew Marty's reputation might be just gossip exaggerated to myth, as envy was as much a marker of success in Hollywood as income. Bender had spent college summers working on movie sets as a production assistant answering to stressed directors, bullying producers, and temperamental stars; he was not afraid of Marty's persona and reserved judgment of Marty until they met. When they did, Marty was polite, and Bender got a bagel with cream cheese.

Marty's success in television was based on meeting Paul Henning, who not only had a brilliant idea for a sitcom *The Beverly Hillbillies*, but could write every show, saving Marty a fortune on writers. Marty also got him to write an episode for the show's stars in which their character died in an automobile accident on Pacific Coast Highway. When a star demanded an unreasonable raise, Marty showed him the script.

Marty carried a muscular torso on short spindly legs. His face, slightly pudgy with a boxer's nose, gave no clues of his origin. If someone asked him if he was Jewish, he stared until the asker regretted asking. He wore his thin blond hair in a silly comb-over but there was no one brave enough to tell him. Marty rarely smiled but when he did it tended to relieve and disarm people. In the Uffizi Museum in Florence, Bender saw Raphael's portrait of Pope Leo X. He recognized Marty immediately.

When Marty's current film wrapped, he often took his leading lady, or if she wasn't willing, someone who was, to Palm Springs for a weekend of tennis, dinners, and sunburned love. There was a joke going around at Hillcrest Country Club that when Marty finished a horror movie about killer spiders, he brought the star *araneae* to The Racquet Club in a jar.

Bender pitched his pilot idea, Marty liked it, they took it to Michael Eisner in a meeting brokered by Navitz. Eisner got his former assistant at ABC to pay Bender to write a pilot script, Marty got a producing fee and switched his agent from William Morris to Navitz Artists.

In script meetings Marty, bored with plot points and character nuance, diverted the conversation to stories about his favorite subject: himself. Bender listened to Marty with the attention of Scheherazade's king. There was the actor who kept calling Marty at MGM:

"Finally, I took his call: who are you and what do you want?"

The guy says, "Marty, it's Baron."

"Do I know you?"

"How could you forget?"

"Forget what?"

"I hear you're starting a film. You promised me a job."

"Really? Where did this conversation take place?"

"In your bedroom after we had sex."

"Describe my bedroom. And the sonofabitch did, right down to the portrait of my mother over the fireplace. Turns out my butler was cruising Santa Monica Boulevard while I was in Palm Springs, pretending to be me, picking up guys, bringing them to the house, and promising them parts in my movies."

Bender, truly impressed, said, "What did you do?"

I said, "I'm sorry, pal, you've been fucking my maid."

Bender's pilot was produced but didn't make the schedule. Nonetheless, Marty and Bender developed a mutually beneficial relationship: Marty asked Bender to read a screenplay and give him notes. In return, Marty let him use his tennis court.

Bender was tennis obsessive. He took lessons with the Olmedo brothers at the Beverly Hills Hotel, hit thousands of backhands against walls, carried a wrist strengthener, and subscribed to *Tennis* magazine. Twice a year he enrolled for a week of private lessons at John Gardiner's Tennis Resort in Carmel.

"So, Mr. Bender, what needs work today?"

"My serve. Also my forehand. And my volley."

"How long have you been taking lessons?"

"Since I was six years old."

"Okay, let's get started. We'll hit a few then we'll see what we can improve."

"Also my backhand."

Bender always played better after a lesson, but because he started from such a low level his improvement would be Darwinian; he estimated he would need to live another ten thousand years to evolve from *okay* to *good*, maybe another fifteen thousand to get *really good*. But *okay* wasn't enough in show business tennis circles, so Bender confined his games with Steve to the public courts in Rancho Park and continued his lessons at the Beverly Hills Hotel.

Holmby Hills was a piece of expensive real estate along Sunset Boulevard between Beverly Hills and Bel-Air. Marty's Tuscan mansion had all the trimmings: screening room, gym, wine cellar, library, professional kitchen, and an outdoor dining patio shaded by giant avocado trees. "Take as many as you like," Marty said. "They just rot."

Marty led him under the grape arbor, past the swimming pool, through the rose garden, down the steps to a covered pavilion overlooking the most beautiful tennis court Bender had ever seen. Surrounded by towering eucalyptus trees on the deuce side and Marty's mansion on the other. Bender stared at the court, he felt its aura, its divinity, it was a holy place; Seneca's Scythian Glade, Oedipus' sacred grove at Colonus, the Temple Mount. Amidst the rustle of the eucalyptus leaves he heard the voice of Bud Collins, "Bender, gaze upon this court. On it you will improve. On it will occur the mutation that will allow you to skip countless generations and propel you to *really good* in your lifetime. Don't fuck this up."

"Hey, Bender. Where are you? You listening to me?" Marty said.

"Sorry. I was admiring the court. You were saying?"

"Here's the drill: You call Theo; if nobody is playing, you can use it. The pool's off limits. You bring your own tennis balls."

After lunch Marty returned to his office where he worked until seven. The court was Bender's unless Theo made an unexpected appearance in the pavilion. He delivered the bad news as a butler should, with a mixture of regret and cruelty.

"Mr. Ransohoff is on his way home, he'll be playing with Warren Beatty, you have to vacate immediately," Theo said.

"Sure," Bender said, figuring there was no point in being Warren Beatty if you can't kick someone off a tennis court.

Bender's skills on Marty's court improved exponentially; his serves landed deeper, bounced higher, he heard the orgasmic pong of the ball hitting the sweet spot on his racquet more often, he was on his way to *really good*. Invitations would follow to play with Hollywood royalty, Bender returning serves from bankable stars, guarding the net in mixed doubles with Oscar-nominated actresses. The day was not far off when he would be able to brag that he was the best tennis player who was a writer and the best writer who was a tennis player. Alex Olmedo noticed the change. "You were good today, champ, you moved me around the court pretty good."

Eventually, as in most matters, Bender found a way to fuck it up.

It began when his lawyer friend Dennis called him.

"You know what I like about you, Bender?"

"No."

"You can keep a secret."

"Okay."

"Are you playing tennis these days?"

"Yes."

"Are you any good?"

"I'm okay."

"I have a friend who likes to play tennis."

"No shit, Dennis. Can you make this conversation any more boring? I'm pretty busy."

"He's in L.A., he's looking for a game. Maybe you could play with him."

"Do I know him?"

"Maybe. He works in the subway."

"I don't know any subway workers."

"Go figure. He likes being underground."

It had to be Abbie Hoffman. "What's he doing in L.A?"

"They're making a movie out of his book. He's working with the writers. I told him about you; he wants to play tennis with you."

"Fine. How will this be arranged?"

"He'll call you. I gave him your number. His cover name is Barry Freed."

"Got it."

"Don't tell anyone."

"Tell anyone what?"

"Atta boy."

After the Chicago 7 trial, Abbie continued political activism, organizing demonstrations against the CIA, Contras, Monsanto, two Republican Conventions, and dropping balloons filled with pig's blood on the floor of the New York Stock Exchange. Articulate, funny, rock 'n' roll-handsome, he made the cover of *Rolling Stone* twice. Although the press sometimes portrayed him as the 'clown of the revolution' he was deadly serious in his dedication to overthrow the military-industrial state and achieve justice for the oppressed. Abbie's commitment to the 'revolution' brought him to the attention of like-minded rock stars and European culture ministers. Just when there was talk of a political career, he was arrested for selling cocaine to an undercover New York policeman. His lawyer prepared Abbie for the worst, he would likely be convicted. With that in mind, Abbie, out on bail, disappeared. Over the years there were sightings, rumors placed Abbie in France, Cuba, Algeria. Another said that he had plastic surgery, burned off his fingerprints and was teaching kindergarten in Long Island. And now, he would be Bender's tennis partner on Marty Ransohoff's court.

Bender parked at the corner of Sweetzer and Fountain, a neighborhood of old apartment buildings; perfect for stashing a mistress or housing a fugitive. A man in tennis whites holding a racquet rapped on his window. Bender opened the door.

"Abbie?"

"I'm Barry now. Barry Freed."

"Cool."

He nodded and got in the car.

Bender wondered if he should have said 'right on' instead of 'cool.'

Abbie's racquet was a vintage Jimmy Connors T2000 Wilson, a formidable weapon in the hands of a pro twenty years ago. Bender's own custom strung Babolat AeroPro was in the back seat, ready to mark him a class enemy. As they drove west along Santa Monica Boulevard, Bender wondered if he would have recognized Abbie from the FBI posters in the Beverly Hills post office. The neatly bearded man sitting next to him still owned a chiseled face. The hair was different; the long Mick Jagger page boy was now a curly mop. This Abbie wore thick tortoise shell frames. "I'm still 20-20," Abbie said. "The lenses are clear. But my nose is different." They drove into Beverly Hills, along Sunset Boulevard, lined with mansions, the dead and departed movie star owners still listed on Maps to the Stars' Homes, turned into Carolwood Drive, and parked in front of Ransohoff's mansion. Bender led Abbie to the carport, they squeezed between a Mercedes 380 SL and a Jaguar XJ6. Bender opened a gate into the rear gardens.

"People home?" Abbie asked, pointing to the cars.

"No, the Rolls is gone," Bender said.

"Nice pool."

"It's off limits."

"Who owns this place anyway?"

"Marty Ransohoff. A producer. He's made some big movies."

Bender was feeling defensive. If Abbie asked him to name one of Marty's movies, would it be the one about mutant killer spiders? Could he frame it as a commentary on the evils of corporate agriculture? Bender was uneasy walking through a rich Hollywood producer's landscape with Abbie. If this was a people's republic Marty would surely be arrested and tried, the Rolls-Royce introduced as evidence, and Marty condemned to a lifetime of shoveling pig manure in a reeducation center in Burbank. When they reached the pavilion Abbie whistled. "Wow, this court is out of fucking sight. You get to play here whenever you want?"

"Not whenever. But enough."

Abbie had been on the Brandeis tennis team; he was that good and would be better if a policeman's horse hadn't stepped on his ankle in a demonstration. Abbie still had a strong first serve that could be followed by a nasty spinning second one. Fortunately, Bender had just returned from a week at John Gardiner's where he majored in nasty spinning serves and combined with his improvement on Marty's sacred court, they split two sets.

Afterwards they toweled off in the pavilion.

"Why can't we use the pool?" Abbie asked.

"I don't know. Rules."

Abbie frowned. "Fucking rules."

On the way back to West Hollywood, Abbie explained that a director had bought his book, Universal paid for a screenplay, and arranged for Abbie to come to Los Angeles to work with the screenwriter.

"He wants it to be accurate. But here's the thing, I'm wanted by the FBI, I'm working in Hollywood. Is that so hard to find out? Or, if they can't, what does that say about the competency of the FBI? Maybe they do know where I am. Did they make a deal with Universal? Nobody tells me anything. Can I relax? Can I stop looking over my shoulder, eat in restaurants, go to a Dodgers game, and not be so paranoid or is the FBI just incompetent?"

"You're in Hollywood, stick with paranoid."

Driving away, Bender thought playing tennis with Abbie might get him points in the revolutionary struggle with

Ellen, who had once said, "I do more for humanity in one day than you do all year in Hollywood." Now Bender could say, "Oh, yeah? Guess who I played tennis with for the revolution?"

Even thinking about Ellen was depressing. Bender confessed to Dr. Grotstein that he was growing tired of living his life in the hope that the people he met, movies stars, writers, directors, and now, a Chicago 7 hero would make him more desirable to his gone wife. Dr. Grotstein said Bender was making progress.

A week later, Abbie got in Bender's car carrying a new Babolat racquet.

"I also brought a bathing suit just in case," he said.

"Out of the question."

"He'll never know."

"The butler will tell him."

Bender invited Steve to play with them, winner stays on the court, introducing Abbie as an old friend from New York. The next time they played Steve brought his wife Dottie, so they could play doubles. Abbie and Dottie teamed up against Bender and Steve and beat them easily.

"You know what I'd like?" Abbie said. "Let's all have dinner Saturday night. I heard you're a pretty good cook, Bender."

"He's better than pretty good," Dottie said.

"Sure. Saturday."

"I'll bring a salad," Dottie said.

After Dottie and Steve left, Abbie said, "If you want to invite a few more people who are cool, it's cool. I want you to meet Johanna. I told her all about you."

"But I'll be introducing you as Barry Freed, correct?"

"Not a good idea. What if someone recognizes me?"

"Would you be comfortable if people knew who you are, when they get there?"

"Better. We're leaving on Monday anyway. It's safer if they know it's me, but don't know my cover identity."

"Huh?"

"They say they met Abbie Hoffman, so what? They say they met Barry Freed who is really Abbie Hoffman my cover is blown."

"Got it. You up for one more set?"

During the Friday run-through of his sitcom Bender reread his guest list. Bender's usual inclination was to ask Ellen, hoping that an evening with Abbie would lead to a reconciliation. Then he remembered an argument they had about political tricksters; dinner with Abbie might have the opposite effect. Abbie's partner Johanna was a ceramicist, so the better choice was Elyn Zola, a site-specific artist who carved faux fossils on canyon walls and then 'discovered' them in the Borrego Badlands. He also invited Mimi and Paul, and his tennis partners, Steve and Dottie. Bender considered vows of silence, sworn on the lives of their children, at least until Abbie left town. He recalled the scene in *Shoot the Piano Player* when a French gangster swears on his mother's life. Truffaut cuts to an old woman falling dead off her rocking chair. None of Bender's friends could keep dinner with Abbie Hoffman a secret. Bender imagined Beverly Hills children falling off their swings like autumn leaves.

The day of the dinner party Bender drove to Bay Cities in Santa Monica, bought Bolognese sauce, pesto, linguini, bread, cheesecake, and fresh basil to leave on the counter to indicate he had made the pesto from scratch.

o   o   o

"I've got a good group of people coming and none of them will call the FBI, but I can't guarantee they won't tell anyone down the road," Bender said.

"I don't care. I'll be gone by then. I'll just be a rumor. Do I really have to join the Writers Guild?"

"You want residuals?"

"Of course."

"Join. Your serve."

o   o   o

Bender introduced Abbie and Johanna to his guests. Mimi whispered to Bender, "He doesn't look like Abbie Hoffman."

"He's had work," Bender said.

During dinner they talked about art, Johanna showed photographs of her ceramic plates with texts relating to hunger issues. One of them said, "If you can read this, you have eaten too much." Mimi read a passage from her new short story about a lousy weekend in Palm Springs with Jim Morrison, and a comedy writer named David.

"I don't want criticism, just tell me how much you love it." When she finished, Elyn said, "Okay, I love it, but shouldn't you give Jim Morrison a pseudonym?"

Mimi shook her head. "No."

Bender was David in the story. Mimi had changed his last name, but he wasn't famous and there was no point in mentioning his real name.

In the end it was just a dinner party. Bender received compliments on his two homemade pasta sauces. All topics of interest to a group of Los Angelenos and the visiting fugitive couple were covered: movies, sports, politics, religion. Out of sensitivity to the revolutionary perspective of Abbie and Johanna, no one complained about their portfolios or business managers. Bender urged Abbie to talk about life on the run.

"It's about staying active, trying to change the world, being political while swimming underwater," Abbie said. "It's a lower profile, but we're okay."

Johanna told how they had toured Europe with forged credentials that identified them as food critics for *Time* magazine. "We ate our way across France in three-star restaurants for free," Abbie said.

"Typical Abbie," Paul said.

After desert, they went out to the deck, passed joints, stretched out on chaises, and stared at up at a rare smog-free night sky.

"Tell the story about the flute, Bender," Dottie said.

"What's that?" Abbie said.

"Nothing."

"Tell it," Johanna said.

"Go on, Bender. We're all sworn to secrecy."

"Not me," Mimi said. "If it's any good, I'm stealing it."

"Okay," Bender said. "I'm at the Troubadour bar, I start talking to an Italian woman, Constanza. She's a cross between Sophia Loren and Monica Vitti. Somewhere in the conversation I mention that I play the flute. She grabs my arm, whispers into my ear that she loves the flute, she would readily give herself to a man who plays it well. I invited her back to my house, where she is expecting me to play for her. I'm just a beginner; I can barely get through 'Old McDonald.'"

Bender noticed a disapproving look on Johanna's face. Was he wandering into a feminist minefield? He didn't say Constanza had a great body. She was gorgeous and flute players turned her on, that's all. "We came out here; I told her to stretch out on a chaise and look up at the stars. Like we're doing now. I got my flute, put on a CD of Rampal playing his unaccompanied *Ave Maria*. I stood right there on the other side of the sliding door. I pretended I was playing."

"Did it work?"

Bender shrugged yes.

Abbie laughed, but Johanna scowled. Bender considered telling her that screwing Italian women with a fake flute was better than screwing French restaurant owners with fake credentials.

"Do you have a pool?" Abbie asked.

"There's a hot tub."

Abbie cocked his head at Johanna. It was her decision.

"Authentic Japanese. Wood. Natural," Mimi added.

Paul said, "You've been in it?"

"Who hasn't?" Mimi said.

Bender led them around the corner of the house. The water was brown and steamy; it looked like a giant bowl of hot miso soup. He brought them towels and returned to his friends.

"Abbie Hoffman. I'm impressed." Lenore said, "He's wanted by the FBI, right? Can you tell us how this happened?"

He leaned into his co-conspirators, "Before I do, you have to swear to secrecy."

"Why?" Mimi said, "They don't exactly sound like Bonnie and Clyde."

o   o   o

When everyone had left, Bender returned to the hot tub. Abbie and Johanna were sitting on the bench, wrapped in towels.

"You have a nice place, here," Abbie said.

"Thanks."

"So what is it like to live in the maw of the mind-fucking capital of the world?" Johanna said.

Bender told them a story that wasn't his but came in useful for such moments. "There was this famous sitcom writer. He took his family to Italy, rented a house in Vernazza. He traded his Nikes for sandals, had his coffee every morning at a café in the piazza, carried a Moleskine notebook with a fountain pen. He instructed his wife and children, 'If anyone asks what I do for a living, do not say I write sitcoms. You are to say I am a poet.' Towards the end of their stay the local newspaper announced an episode of *Mia Madre La Machina* and listed him as the writer. That night a television was set up in the piazza, the entire village came and watched the show. Afterwards, they paraded to his house. The Mayor presented him with a bouquet of flowers, 'All this time we thought you were just a poet.'"

Abbie smiled. "One more game, tomorrow?"

"Sure, if you can play around noon. Marty's still in Palm Springs."

"I'll meet you there. Johanna can drop me off."

o   o   o

Monday, Bender was working in his Warner Bros. office. Bari poked her head in the door. "Marty Ransohoff's on the phone."

"Marty, how are you?"

"I'll get right to the point. You are eighty-sixed from my tennis court."

"What?"

"You violated my trust. With me you only get one shot. You blew it with your friend."

"I'm sorry, I swear I didn't know he was a fugitive."

"Who?"

"Abbie Hoffman."

"Is that his name?"

"He also goes as Barry Freed."

"What the fuck does that have to do with anything?"

"Did the FBI talk to you? I am so embarrassed."

"FBI? He jumped in my pool. My butler saw him. He was naked."

"I am so sorry."

"You know the rules. The pool is off limits."

"Marty..."

"No appeals allowed, pal." Marty hung up. The court was gone. Bender's Scythian Glade, his Colonus. His improvement. He lowered his forehead on his desk, and cursed Abbie.

Later, Bender thought about Abbie's world: the redistribution of wealth, strong unions, universal health care, not a single homeless person in the richest country in the world, and lots of comedy. And his, Bender's world? He would be the best tennis player in history despite his thirty percent first-serve average, an inability to hit a high volley, his awkward footwork. Bender and Steve, like Borg and McEnroe would be rivals trading Wimbledon trophies. But just for a moment. Bender's heart was with Abbie. They wanted the same world. Marty's court was a small price to pay.

He went back to playing tennis at Rancho Park; his serve withered, his backhand went astray, he hit balls into the adjacent court while players waiting their turn laughed at him.

A few weeks later, Marty called. "Look, I'm willing to revisit the issue of the putz who jumped in my pool which led to your temporary suspension."

Bender suppressed a cry of joy at temporary, but knew Marty wanted something in return.

"I finished your screenplay. I have to say it was pretty good. It's not for me, but it's a movie I'd pay to see." Bender knew that Marty never paid money to see anything, he wouldn't be caught dead buying a ticket. Marty only saw movies in his home screening room or went to premieres.

"That's great, Marty. Coming from you…"

"I know a producer who's looking to shoot a film in Paris. I told him about yours. He'll be at the festival in Cannes."

"I'll go to Cannes."

"Good. What else are you doing these days?"

"I have a rewrite to turn in, then maybe a pilot."

"Will you take a look at something for me?"

"Of course."

"A screenplay. Give me some notes, maybe polish a couple of scenes?"

"Send it over."

Bender called Steve. "I got the court back."

Then he called Ellen. "Did I tell you I played tennis with Abbie Hoffman?"

"Like I give a shit, Bender. He's a clown."

"So what? We need clowns. And I liked him," Bender said.

"Good-bye, Bender."

At therapy the next day Dr. Grotstein didn't see the call as a complete setback. "For once, Bender, you disagreed with her. You may be reclaiming your own opinions. Who knows, one day you might admit to not liking Sylvia Plath."

CANNES

Marty, pleased with Bender's free rewrite, arranged a meeting in Cannes with Tarak Ben Ammar, a Tunisian producer, who would also give him a room in his villa in Cap d'Antibes. Bender stepped off the train in the middle of the Cannes Film Festival, well-armed with his screenplay about an American director in Paris whose French wife leaves him. Disconsolate, the director takes flute lessons to distract himself, eventually falls in love with his flute teacher, while his wife, too late, regrets her decision. Bender had possible financing, a free room, and the possibility that Ellen, seeing their lives portrayed in a sensitive European art film, might return.

Sitting on the waiting room couch, Bender had a view of Ammar on the phone in his office, glancing up at Bender, and ignoring him. Not a wave, not even a raised hand, a nod, 'Sorry, give me a minute.'

Bender allowed himself one more pleading glance at the receptionist. She returned a minimal shrug. The ten minutes flew, he added another five, then five more, got up and walked out of the office. No one pursued him down the hallway, apologizing, asking for forgiveness, clutching his sleeves, begging him to return. As Bender stepped in the elevator it occurred to him that they might have thought he had gone to the bathroom.

On the Croisette, Bender strolled aimlessly past cafes, terrace restaurants filled with women and men making deals, celebrating success, all determined to keep Bender out of the movie business. Should he cross the street, take off his shoes, place them neatly on the sand and walk into the Mediterranean like Dirk Bogarde in *Death in Venice*? Better to get a drink. Bender squirmed his way through tables to the bar of La Mandala, ordered a glass of rosé. He would find someone else to finance his film. The Tunisian producer was reputed to be a control freak, he'd find a way to fire Bender, take the film away, or convert it into a musical for Cher. A better plan came to Bender; screw Cannes, screw Ben Ammar, hike to the train station, collect his luggage from storage, get a train back to Nice, rent a car and enjoy a European vacation; eat in starred restaurants, appetite enhanced by the joints he carried in his hollowed-out red Michelin Guide. Bender spotted Irwin Victor, a William Morris agent, holding court with a cast of interesting looking people at a terrace table. Irwin waved; Bender's mood improved as he made his way to the table. Irwin rose out of his chair, came forward to intercept him, a clear signal that Bender would not be invited to join his friends.

"I assume you're here on business," Irwin said.

"I'm meeting with Tarak Ben Ammar."

"A wonderful guy, I'm seeing him tomorrow. Where are you holed up?"

"On my way to the Carlton, you?"

"I'm staying at Kirk's villa. By now, it's a tradition. Let's have a drink later in the week," Irwin said unconvincingly.

"Sure thing," Bender replied, also unconvincingly.

At the station luggage bin, Bender peered through the mesh fence and spotted his suitcase. He rang the bell, then noticed the sign: *La consigne est fermée jusqu'à demain matin.* Bender was stuck in Cannes for another fifteen hours. No problem, check into a hotel, stroll the Croisette, enjoy a first-class dinner, retire early, pick up his luggage and get the fuck out of Le Dodge. La Dodge? He began his search at The Carlton. A desk clerk politely informed Bender there were no rooms available.

"Perhaps The Grand?" Bender said.

"Of course, Monsieur, you may try." Even with his accented English the subtext was clear: *Are you out of your fucking mind? An empty hotel room in the middle of the Cannes Film Festival?*

Bender thanked him, stopped at the gift shop, purchased a toothbrush kit. Two hours later he had been turned away from seven more hotels. At four of them, clerks were kind enough to accept fresh twenties and phone their colleagues in other hotels, but the verdict was the same, there were no vacant hotel rooms in Cannes.

The evening's premiere at the Palais du Cinema would be starting soon, limousines filled with stars and producers were inching their way to the curb, fans, photographers were flanking the red carpeted walk. Bender saw Irwin Victor wearing a dinner jacket, step out of a taxi.

"We meet again," Irwin said.

"I need a favor. My travel agent screwed up. She didn't book a room for me tonight. Any possibility I could crash at your pal's villa? Just tonight. A couch? Anything."

"I couldn't ask him. Kirk Douglas is a client, agents don't ask clients for favors. It's the other way around. Have you tried The Carlton? Sorry, must run, Polanski's holding a seat for me. Say hello to the family."

Was it too late to return to the Tunisian's office and tell him he had trouble finding the men's room?

o   o   o

The restaurant on the Croisette was almost empty, so Bender was shown to a prized table facing the sea. He looked at his watch. It was eight o'clock, only ten more hours to kill before he could claim his luggage. The waiter brought a menu and the wine list. He read the menu three times, studying it like a contract, narrowing his choices, taking dainty sips of a *kir royale*. He reluctantly gave his order to the captain, then entered a lengthy discussion of the wine list with the somme-lier. It was now eight-thirty, nine and a half hours to go; he hadn't even eaten. Things were looking up. Bender began with *pissaladière*, followed by a cold artichoke salad, scallops in a basil sauce, finishing with cherries jubilee. The whole meal, including two espressos, cookies, and a long wait for a check only used up an hour.

Along the Croisette past the Palais du Cinema, crews in neon vests swept up debris, stacked the barriers for the next day's screening. Giant posters advertising other people's movies stared down at him. Bender felt lonely, exiled from the film business, he was tired, he wanted a bath, a bed, half a Halcion. He missed Ellen, he wanted her at his side to laugh at his misstep, to find a way out of this mess. Allowing himself another moment of sadness for the sheer pleasure of it and then, as Dr. Grotstein had suggested he do in such situations, he faced the facts; He had consumed a four-hundred-franc meal, was dressed in Armani clothes, and had nowhere to sleep. In short, he was a rich vagrant.

Bender walked across the street, found a bench. The wine-dark sea stretched out before him, silent save for the sound of tiny waves slapping the sand, behind him he heard loud music from cruising Ferraris, beeping horns, raspy motor bikes. Could he go horizontal on the bench and pass the night? Did French policemen slap heels with their billy clubs like their American brothers and say move on, pal? What was French for move on? The lyrics of "Under the Boardwalk" floated in momentarily but were erased quickly by the image of being mugged by a gang of tattooed French thugs. Better to resume his search for a hotel room, try to bribe a bellhop for a couch in the lobby where he could sneak a snooze.

Bender took out his new toothbrush and retrieved bits of the two-star meal. Somewhere between a thread of scallop and a spit of cherry skin, Bender had an epiphany: there was a place where he could spend the night, legitimately, comfortably, even amusingly, the Casino La Croisette. A short walk and ten minutes later, Bender handed his passport to a clerk, filled out the registration card, entered the Grande Salle. Under magnificent chandeliers, women in gowns, men in dinner jackets, producers, and actors whose movies hadn't screened yet, played baccarat, roulette, and blackjack. Earlier that evening they had walked up the red carpet, waved at fans, posed for paparazzi, then continued out a back exit of the theatre, having no interest in a film that wasn't theirs. The Casino room was a film set of perfect hair, rich tans, gold Rolexes, overexposed breasts. He was safe, screw Halcion. Was that a James Bond at the baccarat table, shaken or stirred, he couldn't remember. Bender dipped in and out of a blackjack game, not bothering to sit down, losing one, winning three, moving to the roulette table where he bet black, enjoying the ambling of the ball in the roulette wheel as it plunked from slot to slot until it came to rest in twenty-four black. As he pocketed his chips, people started to drift in from the screening. He checked his watch, it was ten thirty, tempus fugit, only seven and a half hours to go. At the bar, he nursed a martini, his back to the mirror for a better view of the room.

A woman on his left said, "American?"

"Does it show?"

"I figured you for Russian. I'm Sherrie."

The woman on his right said, "I don't think you look Russian. I'm Martha."

Sherrie said, "Are you from Hollywood?"

"Yes."

"Do you have a film in the festival?"

"No. Do you?"

"As a matter of fact, we do."

"Ah, you're a producing team. Why don't we get a table, I'd love to hear about it."

Both women were fascinating in their own way. Martha knew the inside scoop on every film in the festival, she delivered her pronouncements on their budgets, chances of box office success, downwards to Bender, she was six-two. Sherrie found everything funny, laughed and spoke in a raspy voice that seemed to jump octaves, but she also spoke perfect French to their waiter. Bender had heard of being in love with two women at the same time, this seemed like a prelude. Bender realized he didn't wish Ellen was with him. Was he getting over his wife? Or was this just another distraction?

"Tell me about your film," Bender said.

"We're documentary producers from D.C." Martha said. "Ours is about a Chesapeake family that's been harvesting oysters for four generations. Now they have to deal with warming waters. We have some interest from Canal+."

"Sounds promising. And I love oysters. Shall we get some?"

"Can we have them with champagne? We'll split the check," Sherrie said.

"Absolutely."

They ate a dozen oysters, then another, drank a bottle of Piper-Heidsieck, followed by quiet time on the balcony overlooking the Mediterranean with a killer joint that Sherrie had stashed in her pocket. In the casino, Bender danced first with Sherrie then Martha, who said it would be more fun if the three of them danced together. They gambled modestly, but when Martha hit three blackjacks in a row, doubling down on each, she said, "I quit. I have enough for a new refrigerator."

They returned to the dance floor, ordered another bottle of champagne, and passed the joint discreetly under the table but no one seemed to care. Bender was writing the story in his head, darting back and forth between the two women, the Tunisian producer, his locked luggage; there were two versions, in one he was producing and directing movies with Martha, and then a quick rewrite in which he was married to Sherrie.

Sherrie said, "Bender, I'm really high, you know what happens when I get high?"

"Actually, I don't."

"I get honest. Marth, we need to tell Bender the truth."

"Do we have to?"

Sherrie leaned over and bunked her forehead against Bender's. Her hair smelled of Herbal Essence, her breasts were resting on his arm, he was losing interest in Martha.

"Fuck it, I'm gonna tell him the truth," Sherrie said.

"No fucking," Martha said.

"Too bad, he's kinda cute."

"You're drunk, Sherrie. I'll tell him."

Bender suddenly felt nervous. Truth in Hollywood usually meant bad news.

Martha said, "There is no film, Bender. We're not documentary producers."

"What are you?"

"Lawyers. We both work in the Department of Agriculture. I'm in Market Services, Sherrie's in Foreign Dairy Products because she speaks French. We wanted to go the Cannes Film Festival, screenings, premiers, receptions, and not be tourists behind the ropes."

Irwin Victor waved. He was alone. Seeing Bender with two women, Irwin started towards them. Bender returned the wave, but also gave him the finger, stopping him in his tracks.

"I'm sorry, Martha, you were saying?" Bender said.

Martha said, "We created a fake production company, produced a fictional doc, did all the paperwork, got accredited as participants in the Cannes Film Festival. Want to see our passes?"

"Didn't the Festival officials want to see the film?"

"Of course. It's a real tragedy that it got held up in customs. Should be here any day."

"Tomorrow's the last day of the Festival."

"Um-hum."

"How did you pull this off?"

Sherrie said, "It was easy. We are lawyers, you know."

Bender told them about walking out of his meeting with the Tunisian producer.

"Definitely self-destructive," Martha said. "You need to take a look at that."

"Don't worry, I'm sure it will work out for the best," Sherrie said.

"It already has," Bender said. "Well, what now?"

"Too bad we checked out. We could have gone back to our hotel room, played Scrabble until dawn, and ordered room service."

"Let's go for a ride." Sherrie said. "We'll take the top down."

o　o　o

Bender squeezed his frame horizontally into the narrow back seat of the Peugeot convertible and stared straight up at the sky. Martha headed north towards Mougins.

"Hey, Bender, do you want to come with us to Monte Carlo?" Sherrie said.

"You have a car in the Grand Prix?"

"Don't be silly. But we are covering it for our boss. He's thinking of remaking *Grand Prix*."

"Who's your boss?"

"Steven Spielberg."

"You're getting full access to the race?"

"Of course."

"Hotel?"

"A suite."

"We'd have to get my luggage first."

"*Pas de problème,*" Sherrie said.

Bender turned around in his seat. The lights of Cannes dimmed and flickered off as dawn spread across the Mediterranean. He was happy in the company of these two lovely con women. Where would they take him next? To the Vatican, as accredited emissaries of Cardinal Hickey with a special visit to the Sistine Chapel, free of tourists, or the papal apartments with a private tour by Il Papa himself? But in the end, they had coffee and croissants in the square in Mougins, with phone numbers exchanged, promises to stay in touch. When the women dropped him off at the train station in Cannes, they waved goodbye from the Peugeot, Bender regretted his decision. Had he walked out of another office? Choices, decisions, they were all made through the lens of not *moving on.* It was no life, he decided, but it was the one he had chosen.

o   o   o

A year later Martha quit the Department of Agriculture and moved to Los Angeles hoping to find a studio job. Bender invited her to stay in his house in Benedict Canyon. He opened the futon couch in his office, eventually they ended up sharing his bed. It wasn't love, but Bender liked the domesticity, he made no demands, they were more roommates than lovers, and when Martha moved out, she was on a fast track to be a development executive for George Lucas. In the last two months of living with Bender, she was also secretly seeing an English director who was attached to direct *Mandrake the Magician.*

Bender ran into Martha at an Academy screening. Martha said she missed Benedict Canyon, his deck, the hot tub, and the view.

"And me?" Bender said.

"Not that much," she laughed and hugged him.

After the film they went to Kate Mantilini's for chili. Martha told Bender that Sherrie was married and had moved back to Michigan.

"Whatever happened to your French screenplay?" Martha said.

Bender shrugged. "It's still out there, looking for a home."

"It's not for George, but if you have anything else let me know."

In his bed Bender missed Martha's soft length. He knew he was a merely a fragment in her calculus of forged documents, cribbed resumes, ambition, beauty, and charm. Cannes, Monte Carlo, Benedict Canyon, Spielberg. At dawn, Bender awakened, in his dreams he had found solutions to life's problems. The neatly stacked pillows on the other side of his bed reminded him that he had spent another night alone. Bender returned to a more familiar, less bearable despair. If Ellen was here, she would have already finished her asanas, and if in the mood, invite him to shower with her and make love amid the swaying loofas.

Why?

Bender tried to recall his dreams, were there any clues to the mystery of his divorce, any that could shed light on why Ellen had left him? Any that he could present to Dr. Grotstein? Bender feared the session when the doctor said, "For God's sake, Mr. Bender, not that again, can't you talk about something else, besides your stupid ex-wife?"

He could. Bender thought. Next week was his birthday, he had planned a big party and wouldn't invite Ellen. Or perhaps he would.

Bender made coffee and walked out on to his deck overlooking Benedict Canyon. There was no sunrise to admire. His deck faced west; the sun rose behind him. Was the hawk floating above him observing his misery or just searching for a plump field mouse?

Bender watched the gray black water of the Pacific turn into an endless shimmering mirror as the sun made its way over the roof of his house. Energized by the view, Bender stretched three ways and took his morning piss over the edge of his deck onto an agave cactus.

BENEDICT CANYON

Stretched out on Dr. Grotstein's green leather couch, his head crunching a paper napkin, his feet dangling over the edge, Bender free associated railroad tunnels in Italy. "Did you know they all have names?" he said.

Bender waited for a response from Dr. Grotstein. There was none.

"I'm on the train from Santa Margarita to Rome along the Mediterranean: I enter the pitch black of a tunnel then emerge into a blinding blue sea and sky. Then bang, I'm in another tunnel, everything goes black."

"Does your tunnel have a name?"

"Yes, *Divorzio Doloroso.*"

In the silence that followed, Bender counted the strings on the spirit catcher hanging on the wall. Eight. "Next week I'm having a birthday party."

"Congratulations."

"I hope it will take my mind off my ex-wife."

There was no response from Dr. Grotstein.

"I'm debating inviting her."

Bender heard what sounded like a belch.
"Excuse me," Dr. Grotstein said.

o   o   o

The day after his birthday party Bender met Dennis and Mimi for a late breakfast in Steve's delicatessen. Dennis pronounced the birthday party a disaster. Mimi disagreed, "I wouldn't say disaster. But you were an idiot to invite that actress."

Alexis Stone. Bender sat next to her at an Emmy dinner, they chatted over the winners and losers, he impulsively invited her to his birthday party. Bender worried that she was too beautiful, out of his league, reserved for stars, powerful agents, studio executives; he was merely a working writer, but he also knew that in Hollywood, where Alexis' looks could quiet an elevator, make Ferrari drivers miss gears, it was in Bender's favor that she was a beauty in a city full of beauties.

Alexis said, "I hate birthday parties."

Bender, neglecting to ask his shipmates to tie him to the mast, replied, "We will be playing pin the tail on the donkey."

"In that case, I accept," she said.

Bender planned to charm Alexis at his party, then woo her with literature as F. Scott Fitzgerald did with Sheila Graham. He pictured them in his bed, making love while kicking old issues of *The New York Review of Books* to the floor, *Editions du Masque* paperbacks crumbling under their sweating bodies; in love, happy, and Ellen jealous. Then what? Would Ellen call to say she had changed her mind?

Probably not, but Bender could rename his tunnel *Alexis Distrazione dal Divorzio.*

The evening of the birthday party, Bender's gardener Maple, a gentle, but often confused hippie, showed up four hours late with flats of fresh impatiens. He was still planting them in front of the picture window with his ass crack in full view as his guests arrived. Later, a waiter walked into a plate glass door but stoically continued to serve the mini tacos with two blood red cotton balls stuffed in his nostrils. Alexis arrived with an actor, a chisel jawed behemoth, who had a recurring role on a hit series, neutering Bender's romantic fantasy. Bender, despondent, shared six long lines of coke in his bathroom with Jimmy and Annette, rendering him impotent an hour later when Alexis got into a fight with her television actor date, asked him to leave, then invited Bender to his bedroom. She whispered obligatory clichés about his abject performance: *don't worry, these things happen, I just want to be held, you probably had too much to drink, there will be another time* then trailed off into a sniffy snore. Bender decided to tell her in the morning they had made wonderful literary love and hope she wouldn't remember.

"Look, the real reason your party sucked was because someone stole your birthday present," Mimi said.

It was Dennis's gift; a finely cast miniature silver flute with a screw-on coke spoon. Bender thought of himself as a user, he was not an addict. He lived by the motto 'Nothing in Excess' inscribed on the temple of Apollo at Delphi and partook of the drug accordingly. Or did he? It was a question he posed to Dr. Grotstein: "Cocaine makes me feel like I got there before I'm there. Is that so bad?"

"What do you think?" Dr. Grotstein said.

"I'm recreational," Bender said.

○   ○   ○

At the table, Dennis asked, "Who do you think stole it?"

"I vote for Alexis or her boyfriend," Steve said.

"Your agent," Mimi said.

"Navitz? Cocaine?" Bender said. "No way. The guy won't take cough medicine. Dennis?"

"The waiter with the bloody nose. I'm a criminal lawyer, I know a thief when I see one," Dennis said.

"Forget the waiter, he's born-again. And the guy with Alexis wasn't her boyfriend. She never goes to parties alone. Anyway, she has a big crush on me."

Bender wasn't exaggerating. Before she left, Alexis agreed to go to Santa Barbara with him the following weekend. Her scene partner in Milton Katselas' Saturday class had booked a commercial and cancelled their rehearsals.

Steve said, "Dennis, why don't you just get Bender another flute spoon?"

"I'll even pay for it," Bender said.

"He doesn't need another spoon. He needs to stop doing coke. Come to a meeting," Mimi said.

"I'm not an addict. I'm recreational."

Dennis pasted cream cheese on his bagel. "The guy who made it lives in Bolinas. All his pieces are one of a kind. It must be a bummer to know one of your friends is a fucking thief."

"I doubt it," Bender said.

"Hey, wait a minute, I forgot, the guy also had a saxophone spoon for sale. I could get it."

"No. I'm a flute player. Thanks to you, Mimi."

○   ○   ○

Coffee after an AA meeting Mimi suggested Bender learn to play a musical instrument. "The discipline and practice will cure you faster than any psychiatrist, believe me. You'll be patient, calm, you'll view change incrementally instead of wanting the quick result. It will help you get over Ellen, maybe get you to Cocaine Anonymous and stop doing blow."

About music as curative, Mimi spoke with authority. Her father Sol was a studio violinist at Fox, equally at home playing Bach concertos and cues for car chases.

"I used to play the trombone," Bender said.

"It's a boy's instrument. You need something adult."

A few days later Mimi called him. "I have a teacher for you. Amy Menish. Call her immediately."

Amy taught in her apartment on the outskirts of Hancock Park. Arriving early, Bender waited at her door, listening to a flute playing scales. The music stopped, a moment later the door opened, a teenage girl emerged. In *Shoot the Piano Player*, Charles Aznavour, a classical pianist on his way to audition for an impresario, passes a young violinist coming out of the office. Bender was happy when his life imitated art, especially if it was by Truffaut.

Amy was in her thirties, bouncy short, dressed in a floppy sweater and Indian drawstring pants. When she played, she took a big breath, dipped low then came up high into the music, like a pitcher winding up before throwing a fastball. Amy did studio jobs, played at local jazz clubs, was a ringer in a doctors' orchestra. She gave Bender a loaner flute. "No point in buying one until you really commit to the instrument. Here's how you hold it, Oh, that's good. You have the posture, very strong breath. Tell me you do yoga."

After the first lesson (how to hold the flute and position the lips on the mouthpiece) Bender left, carrying Amy's flute in a black leather case. More of *Shoot the Piano Player*: the young violinist who comes out of the office is crying. Aznavour realizes she may have had sex with the impresario to advance her career, which is what Aznavour's wife will do later in the film to advance his. Aznavour goes on to become a famous pianist, but his wife, consumed by guilt, jumps out of a window. Bender searched for the lesson in his own life but came up empty.

At the conclusion of the second lesson (basic fingering) Bender announced his commitment to the flute. After the third lesson (long tones) Amy took him to a house on Rodeo Drive where a retired oncologist sold him a used Gemeinhardt flute. After the fourth lesson (C major scale) Amy made tea and said as much as she was tempted, there was a boyfriend, Jeff, a trumpet player at Harrah's in Tahoe.

"He's giving it one more year, then he'll move back to LA with enough cash for a condo and me."

He quickly progressed from "Old MacDonald" to "Ode to Joy," then "Für Elise." Used to getting there before he got there, he took no pleasure in mastering tone, breath control or playing notes slowly. Scales bored him, interval exercises were tiresome, "Für Elise" became nightmarish; he searched his storage unit, brought home vinyls of Hubert Laws, Herbie Mann, and Bud Shank. Bender played along, fitfully, imagined their notes coming from his flute. He discovered *Music Minus One*, recordings of accompanists without the soloist, the second movement of Mozart's Concerto for Flute and Orchestra was within reach if he skipped the cadenza. Amy had seen this behavior before.

"It won't work," she said. "Playing the flute is like anything else, you have to learn the basics before you move on to the fun stuff."

Bender tried; he played long notes slowly until he felt he would go mad, then like an addict, hit Bud Shank on his turntable and bopped along, sputtering, missing notes, silent on Bud's nimble solos. With Herbie Mann's band he was a sideman, nodding to scattered applause, wandering offstage during Philly Joe Jones' drum solo, and sneaking a line of coke before he came back for the chorus. Bender didn't care that he only played twenty per cent of the notes. Amy said his playing was getting worse not better.

o   o   o

Bender couldn't decide if his weekend with Alexis in Santa Barbara was a success or a further descent into a relationship that already had the scent of disaster. To begin, Alexis needed no literary help. She belonged to three book clubs, subscribed to the *London Review of Books*, *Granta*, *The Paris Review* and, unfortunately, *The Journal of Past Lives*. In the middle of the night, she told Bender they had been unhappily married in Vincennes and tearfully confessed to an affair with Louis VII. Alexis saw no reason why it would be different in this one, there would always be a French aristocrat or an A-list director waiting for her. Bender nodded, went back to sleep.

In Los Angeles, Alexis moved in and out of his Benedict Canyon house, disappearing for days. On the checkout line at Gelson's, Bender saw a photograph of Alexis on the cover of *People*, emerging from the Pacific in Maui, holding hands with a famous actor.

"Relax, Bender, he's gay," she said. "His agent needed a photo shoot to show he's dating."

Alexis wanted children, she didn't want children, she alternately loved/hated him, she went to Lakers games but avoided parties and screenings.

"There are going to be a lot of industry people there and I don't want to be seen as a couple."

"But we are a couple."

"Privately."

"What am I, some jerk with a WGA card?"

"That's the point, you're a writer. You make people nervous. Writers are always trying to sell something."

She was right. Bender couldn't meet with his podiatrist without telling him about an unsold screenplay buried in his drawer, or an idea for a television show. His director friends only agreed to lunch with Bender if he promised not to pitch anything.

Alexis continued, "And you're not gay so they'll see us as a couple."

"But we are."

"We are and we aren't."

"How am I supposed to know when?"

"You'll feel it."

Bender did, never more acutely when Alexis returned from an audition describe with Proustian recall, the receptionist, the waiting room, then the names, ages, makeup, credits of the competing actresses, what they wore, and finally the audition itself.

"The director wanted a nervous housewife. I hope I gave him an anxious housewife. There is a difference, right? Can I show you the nervous housewife? Okay, here's the anxious housewife. Which do you like better?"

The odds of getting the job were slim, when Alexis got the news that someone else was cast, she sunk into depression, self-doubt, and bruised narcissism, finding solace in tormenting Bender.

"I told Milton about you after class. He said you are projecting negativity, and your envy is toxic. He says you need to get clear with your own failure and not try to impose it on me. It's why I'm not booking commercials. He wants you to come to the Scientology Center. He'll help you. And you need to read his book."

Bender was aware that her auditions were not for a chance to play Blanche Dubois or Lady Macbeth but rather a housewife who tells her neighbor about a better bleach. He recalled a closeted misogynist but publicly feminist producer telling him, "Never date an actress. They are fucking crazy. But if you do, it's better if she's a star."

One night between shots of Cuervo Gold and a tic-tac-toe of coke lines, Alexis grabbed Bender's collar and pulled him in for a close-up. Her breath was a package of everything Bender knew he shouldn't be doing, including the tiny smidge of white dust on her nose, but he was in love and didn't care.

"Bender," she said, "there is one thing about you that if you could change, I would love you madly forever."

"Tell me what it is, I'll change."

Alexis told him.

Bender said, "I can do that. I can."

The next morning, Bender nudged her soft shoulder, "Last night, you said there was one thing I should change, and if I did, you'd love me forever. What was it?"

"I don't remember."

Why Bender remained in this dumb relationship was a question to Dr. Grotstein at his next appointment.

"Okay, I understand that my obsession for Alexis is inflamed by her ambivalence, her refusal to commit, I see that."

"That's good, that's progress," Dr. Grotstein said.

Bender sighed. "It was my refusal to let go. To move on. I need to change. It's the same with Ellen. The idea of the relationship is more important than the actual woman."

"I like what I'm hearing, Mr. Bender."

"Maybe couples' therapy would help."

"With whom?"

"Both?"

Dr. Grotstein said, "Here's another idea. Why don't you just leave that poor woman alone?"

He did. At last, out of the tunnel of *Alexis Distrazione dal Divorzio*, Bender put aside his flute shortcuts and rededicated himself to long tones, scales, and arpeggios. He turned down invitations from Hubert Laws to play along on his "Gymnopédie #1," returned Rampal, Shank, and *Music Minus One* to storage. His playing improved. He finished a screenplay, left it to marinate in his Commodore for another week. Dr. Grotstein suggested there might be light at the end of the therapy tunnel, at some sacrifice to himself, as Bender's payments helped support the repairs to Jasper, a restored 1950 Jaguar XK120 so named by Dr. Grotstein, an eccentricity Bender overlooked.

"Continue on this path, I see the possible termination of our work. I will miss you, but there is one last issue we should address."

"What's that?" Bender said.

"Your use of cocaine."

"It's not a problem. I'm recreational."

"As you wish. Jasper needs another water pump."

"My cocaine habit is supporting your car's water pump habit?"

"Precisely."

"That doesn't sound right."

"Blame British engineering. I'm afraid our time is up. See you next week."

CUERNAVACA

Still bothered by his psychiatrist calling out his affection for cocaine, Bender nevertheless accepted a phone call from his lawyer friend Dennis, who made a living defending drug dealers. "I have a client, first name Eric, a Stanford MBA who moved tons of weed in and out of Stanislaus County. Thanks to me he managed not to end up in jail. He retired, moved to Cuernavaca with his family. He's selling his house and returning to the states. He's throwing a big farewell party. Want to come along?"

"It's in Mexico, right?"

"You flunk geography? Where else?"

"I'm not sure." Memories of Ellen and the beach in Puerto Vallarta returned.

"Mexico has some painful memories for me."

"Annette's coming."

On the other hand, Bender thought, Cuernavaca was inland, it was the setting of Malcolm Lowry's *Under the Volcano* and there was the possibility of sharing a room with Annette.

"Okay," Bender said.

Mimi's uncle was an editor at Fox, who, like other Hollywood artists and writers moved his family to Cuernavaca during the blacklist. His daughter, Mirandi, still lived there.

"You should call my cousin, Bender," Mimi said, "She's great, knows the best people. But you must bring her a Hebrew National salami."

The day before they were supposed to leave, Annette phoned. "I can't go with you. I just got a listing in Bel-Air, and I need to stage the house ASAP if I want to show it this weekend. It's listed at six million, so do the math." Bender made an exception and did it: at six percent Annette would earn a $360,000 commission.

Bender met Dennis at LAX, they flew to Mexico City and checked into the Camino Real Hotel. Seeking cultural absolution in advance of what promised to be a depraved weekend in Cuernavaca, they spent the morning at the Museum of Archaeology, the afternoon visiting the homes of Frida Kahlo, Diego Rivera, and Leon Trotsky. Dennis, who came from a long line of Bronx Trots, cried at his gravesite, and bought Trotsky ballpoint pens in the gift store. Bender, whose grandfather was a Brooklyn Stalinist, was unmoved. The next day Dennis hired a driver to take them to Cuernavaca.

Whether Dennis was attempting to confound the DEA tapping his phone or simply abusing his client's products, a common condition of lawyers representing drug dealers, almost everything he told Bender about the weekend was wrong.

"No, Eric's not selling his house. His wife is in real estate, she's got the listing and decided to throw a party, invite a lot of potential buyers to show off the house."

"Is Eric getting out of the drug business?"

"Don't ask."

"Is he moving back to America?"

"That's another question you don't have to ask."

"The guy who's selling the house? Is he in drugs?"

"Big time."

"How come I'm allowed to know that?"

"I don't know."

The day of the party Eric had a full day of tennis, Brenda was busy with the caterers, leaving Bender and Dennis to explore Cuernavaca. In the gift shop at The Palace of Cortes, he bought postcards, a poster of Diego Rivera's epic mural, and a tin statue of the Infant Jesus of Prague to add to his collection. Bender phoned Mirandi, introduced himself, told her he had a gift from Mimi.

"Oh, my God, a Hebrew National, right? Come right over," she said. "Take a taxi, you'll never find it."

Mirandi was a Berkeley graduate in her sixties, morphed into a *dama distinguida*. She wore a white cotton shirt over white pants, no makeup on her sun-browned skin, her silver hair pulled back in a tight bun. If she had a machete, she would be a *campesina* in the Diego Rivera mural.

"Come outside, guys, we'll have drinks." She led them through the house, passing a Tamayo canvas, Orozco woodcuts, Buñuel film posters, religious masks, and a shelf of pre-Colombian figurines. Bender, who did not share Hollywood's fixation on the young to the exclusion of the old, immediately fantasized *matrimonio* to this Jewish-Mexican revolutionary. He saw them making dawn love in the carved fourposter, then padding off to his office, a thermos of *champurrado* waiting on his desk, where he would write his screenplay about Pancho Villa. A moment later, this scenario collapsed. Mirandi's husband strode onto the patio, wearing a "Free Leonard Peltier" T-shirt, cargo shorts, gray dreadlocks bouncing off his sculpted shoulders.

"Guys, say hello to Lou, my best fella."

Mirandi served mezcal and Doritos under a canopy of pink bougainvillea. "I know Doritos are gross, but I became addicted to them when we lived in Los Angeles. Are you guys in the party?"

Did she mean Brenda's upcoming real estate gala or the Communist Party? Bender chose the latter. "I'm unaffiliated. Is there still a Communist Party in Los Angeles?"

"You'd be surprised," Lou said, "the party's got a lot to say to the problems in America. We don't go in for the old labels anymore; we keep a low profile."

Mirandi said, "My father joined at the height of the blacklist. We found out later that the baker at Cantor's Deli, who was the party secretary, figured he had to be an undercover FBI agent. What idiot would join the Communist party now? He never entered his name, just pocketed the initiation fee, and my father was never officially a member. But Fox blacklisted him anyway, so we moved here."

"And you stayed?"

"Had to. I met Lou. He was a Panther on the run, love at first sight." She poured another round of mezcal. "Mimi told me you're a writer, Bender, what about you, Dennis?"

"I'm his lawyer."

"When I was in college, I wanted to be one," Mirandi said. "But my father told me there would be no need for lawyers in Soviet America."

CUERNAVACA

Postcards from Cuernavaca

Dear Mimi,
Cuernavaca is beautiful. Big party tonight. Your cousin is terrific; she loved the salami. Served mezcal and Doritos.
Bender

Dear Dr. Grotstein,
Cuernavaca is beautiful. Wonderful museums, great food, I'm relaxing and thinking a lot about our last session.
Bender

Dear Alexis,
Cuernavaca is beautiful. Visited Frida Kahlo's house. Talk about feminists! Let's have dinner and discuss when I get back. Be good to see you, catch up. I miss you and am feeling a lot clearer.
Love, Bender

Dear Ellen,
Cuernavaca is beautiful. Visited Frida Kahlo's house. Talk about feminists! Let's have dinner and discuss when I get back. Be good to see you, catch up. I miss you and am feeling a lot clearer.
Love, Bender

o   o   o

The night of the party, armed security guards checked Bender and Dennis's names at the entrance to the hacienda then waved their taxi through the open iron gates. Its white-washed walls and balconies were illuminated by hundreds of candles in hanging lanterns. The house was alive, it glimmered, shook, flickered from second to second. Who had owned this property, Bender wondered. Jay Gatsby? Charles Foster Kane? Augustin Meaulnes? Inside, people danced to a DJ, waiters followed waiters carrying trays of unending food, there were bar stands in every corner where handsome mixers constructed *Mojitos*, *Margaritas*, *Daiquiris*, and, new to Bender, *Los Penicillins*. Brenda had staged the house: removed all the furniture and emptied two Cuernavaca art galleries to decorate the walls. People had to stand, dance, or imagine their own décor if they bought it.

Brenda found Bender, took his hand. "Come with me. I want you to meet some terrific people." She introduced him to a couple from Mexico City, he was in oil, she was a lawyer, a Swiss banker, a plastic surgeon, and his wife, just back from Vail, a Mexican movie star he didn't recognize, and the owner of the largest grossing McDonald's in Morelos. Everyone agreed that it was a great party then politely resumed their conversation in Spanish. Bender mumbled an excuse, slipped away to a bar, and ordered another *Los Penicillin*, a drink he was beginning to like.

Dennis found him. "Ready?"

"For what?"

"Follow me."

Brenda's husband Eric was waiting for them at a door. He tapped out a combination on a security pad; they entered a wine cellar that was larger than Bender's living room in Benedict Canyon. "It's also a safe room," Eric said. "Food, water, telephone, weapons, air-conditioning, not to mention a direct line to the US Consulate."

A silver tray of wine glasses, a row of dusty wine bottles sat on a long narrow wooden table. Two young Mexican men, one wearing a Joy Division T-shirt, the other a Ralph Lauren pink polo, with cashmere sweaters over their shoulders welcomed them. Gentlemen of means, intelligence, and charm; hip narco-traffickers, not to be fucked with.

"Say hello to Bender, guys," Dennis said.

Joy Division said, "I'm Rodolfo, this is my associate Jorge, you know Eric, of course."

"I hope you like wine," David said.

"I do."

"It's your house, Rodolfo?" Bender said.

"Yes."

"I'll tell you right now if I had the money, I would buy it and not change one thing. It is perfect."

"You are kind to say so."

Jorge filled wine glasses, "Shall we sit? Here, we are partial to Italian. The Super Tuscans, the manly Barolos." He reached for an empty bottle, already decanted, held it out like a newborn, "May I present a 1970 *Antinori Solaia?*"

Bender was wine ignorant. At supermarkets he had three requirements: red, under ten dollars, and if he bought two bottles, he expected to get one free. Though he drank vintage wines in Beverly Hills restaurants, he had never tasted traces of blackberry, red currant, vanilla, chocolate, cut hay, leather, tobacco, or chalky soil, no matter what the sommelier said. But he knew the ritual: he swirled the wine in his glass, held it to the light, studied, sniffed, took a mouthful, silently gargled, then swallowed. "Magnificent," he said.

A *Barolo* (superb) and a *Lamoresca* (enchanting) followed the *Antinori*. The three glasses of wine added to the five earlier *Los Penicillins* tipped Bender over; he was drunk. What about the coke? He whispered to Dennis, "We came all this way to drink wine?"

Rodolfo smiled, took a blue sugar bowl from a shelf and placed it on the table.

"This will be uncut Bolivian," Rodolfo said, pushing twenty thousand dollars of cocaine under Bender's nose.

What now? Bender searched the table. There was no spoon, no mirror, no straw, his pinky nail was trimmed too short for a dip into the bowl. Reach into his wallet and roll up a twenty dollar bill? It would be uncivilized in the presence of his elegant hosts.

"After you," Bender said, stalling.

"No, after you."

"I find myself without paraphernalia."

"No problem," Rodolfo said, as he handed Bender a miniature silver flute with a coke spoon screwed into its end. "Be my guest."

Bender stared at the flute spoon, turning it in his hand.

"Exquisite, isn't it?" Rodolfo said.

"Where did you get this?"

"It was a present from a friend in Los Angeles."

"Who?"

"A friend. Do you need his name?"

"When?"

"When?" Rodolfo said.

"Yes. When did your friend give it to you?"

"I don't know, a month ago. What does it matter?"

"What's his name? Is he a gardener, a waiter?"

"I don't think that is your business. Why are you asking me these questions?"

"It's mine."

"I beg your pardon?"

"It's mine. Your friend stole it from me. From my house. At my birthday party."

"You are saying I have a friend who is a thief?" Rodolfo said.

Bender, a closeted coward who aimed to please, a non-confrontational seeker of the middle way, had just insulted a narco-trafficker to his face. Was he fucking insane? Was it the wine? *Los Penicillins?* It couldn't be the cocaine – he hadn't had any. "Fucking right."

Rodolfo tightened his lips and drummed his fingers on the table. Was this the gesture that would precede his execution? Would Bender be hung from an *autopista* bridge? He turned to Dennis, "Didn't you tell me this was one of a kind?"

"Yes," Dennis said.

"So, if it's one of a kind then this must be mine. The one you gave me. The one that was stolen from my house at my birthday party." He turned to Rodolfo, "I'm not accusing you of stealing it."

Rodolfo stared at him. His fingers continued to drum.

"I'm just saying you have received stolen property."

There was silence. Bender had come this far; he might as well go all the way. "And motherfucker, I want the name of the thief who stole it."

There was a chilling silence. Eight seconds. One, two, three, four, five, six seven, eight.

Rodolfo shot an ice-cold stare at Bender, then took a mouthful of wine, swirled it in his cheeks.

"I want the name," Bender said.

Bender had never personally seen a spit-take. He had witnessed them in movies and sitcoms. Rodolfo's mouthful of wine shot out across the table in a fine spray into Bender's face. Dennis doubled up, banging the table in concert shrieking. Jorge had fallen off his chair, he was rolling on the floor, laughing.

"I don't get it. What's so funny?" Bender said, wiping the wine off his nose.

"You tell him," Dennis said to Rodolfo.

Rodolfo was gasping for air. "I can't. You tell him."

"It's yours," Dennis said. "I got the guy in Bolinas to make another one. I gave it to Rodolfo earlier. I told him to pretend it was his."

"If you could have seen your expression when I showed you the flute. Priceless," Rodolfo said.

"Great fucking practical joke, man. Great!" Eric said.

Bender did not like practical jokes. He acknowledged their ingenuity, the planning that went into them, but they were just intricate tricks at someone's expense. Jokes should be unpractical; two guys walk into a bar, not some shit that happens to you when you walk into a bar. "Oh, a practical joke," Bender said. "A good one. Rodolfo, I apologize for calling you a motherfucker."

"I accept."

Rodolfo held out his hand. They shook.

"Well, shall we?" Rodolfo said, pointing to the bowl.

"Tell you the truth, Rodolfo," Bender said, "I am so much in awe of the *Barolo* that I would like another glass. I fear the powder will interfere with the experience *du vin*. Tell me, will I be tasting hints of dark chocolate and lavender?"

Bender and Dennis decided to hike back to Eric's house. It was close to dawn. There was no traffic, they walked in the middle of the empty street.

"So how big are those guys?"

"Rodolfo owns the largest generic drug company in Mexico. You want some knock-off Valium, he's got it."

"Generic? You said he was a drug dealer."

"He is. Oh, you meant a drug dealer. Why would you think that?"

Bender didn't answer. He couldn't remember and he didn't care.

Cocaine makes me feel like I got there before I'm there.

He reached into his pocket, took out the silver flute, unscrewed the coke spoon and tossed it into the gutter.

"Hey, there's a taco stand," Dennis said. "Who knew they have them in Mexico? Breakfast?"

When Bender got home there were two messages on his answering machine: the first was Navitz: "Bender, call me, I found a financial advisor for you." The second was from Ellen: "For Christ's sake, Bender, we're divorced. Get on with your life."

VAN NUYS

Neil Navitz negotiated a deal for Bender to create television shows at Warner Bros. In addition to a hefty weekly salary against profits, an office, and an assistant, he also got a parking spot with his name stenciled on the concrete barrier. Navitz said, "Protect it with your life, Bender, it is your property, your seat in synagogue, do not let friends use it and if you find an unknown car in it, call security."

Navitz grew up in the San Fernando Valley, where his uncle owned a Judaica supply store. After school and Sundays, he helped sell embroidered velvet pouches containing a tallit, tefillin, and personalized yarmulkes; on holidays he sold Hanukah menorahs, Seder plates, Eliyahu cups, Afikomen bags. There were stacks of Hebrew books for children on a table, a shelf devoted to comical statues of shtetl characters borrowed from *Fiddler on the Roof,* CDs of famous cantors, and a selection of Dead Sea cosmetics.

One of his uncle's customers was Milt Ludwig, a senior television agent at William Morris, and an elder at Valley Beth Shalom in Encino. His children's Bar and Bat Mitzvah parties were legendary, Danny's *Star Wars* on the Fox lot, Chelsea's *Wizard of Oz* at MGM, and a *Frisco Kid* barbecue on the Warner Bros. western street. Impressed with Neil's charm and sales ability, Milt urged Neil to call him when he graduated from UCLA. Neil showed up the next day at Milt's office, announced he had quit college, he wanted to start immediately. Neil rose quickly from the mail room to full agent. He had the ability to spot talented young actors and convince them that he could make them movie stars. He was almost six feet tall, in contrast to the old joke about a William Morris agent who brags, "That's my son, look how short he is already." Navitz mastered politeness in the face of rudeness, 'Thank you for returning my call' (*two weeks ago, you prick*) he picked up the math of show business (*net, gross, rolling gross, box office, overhead, package fees, advance against profits, deferred*). Neil memorized credits, dined out every night with important clients, potential clients, studio executives; he refused dinner invitations unless there was someone at the table who had client potential. Two years later, Navitz turned down a raise, a bigger office, a promised partnership, and, along with two other ambitious agents, quit William Morris and founded their own agency, Navitz Artists, with Neil as president. As the agency grew, Navitz, aware of his own truncated education, hired people to transform him into a man of culture, sophistication, and exquisite taste. Saturday mornings were spent in crash courses with USC professors in history, economics, American literature, then afternoons with golf pros in preparation for joining the Bel-Air Country Club. He bought courtside tickets to the Showtime Lakers; to attend a game with Navitz and get a high-five from Magic Johnson was a new sign of Hollywood status. During half-time Navitz dispensed greetings, hugs, and whispers to power members of the industry who congregated on the floor in front of his seat.

As an art collection was essential, Navitz gave an important New York gallery owner a short-lived directing career, to another who wanted to act, small roles in his client's films. Both gallerists steered the best work of contemporary artists to his walls. He told Bender that Mark Rothko 'spoke to him,' he 'read' Bridget Riley, Saul LeWitt made him cry. On the other hand, Navitz had no knowledge of any other contemporary art; a mention of Merce Cunningham, John Cage, or Robbe-Grillet, resulted in an empty stare. Nonetheless, Navitz made a significant contribution to The Museum of Modern Art and gained a seat on the board. If Berenson were alive to lecture him on the late Italian Renaissance Navitz would have gotten him a date with Madonna. But, as Navitz knew well, in the eyes of his fellow board members, the artists whose painting he bought, and his fellow attendees at Davos, he always would be an *agent*, albeit an uber one.

Bender returned his call.

"You now need," Navitz said, "premium financial assistance; not just an accountant to do your taxes but a business manager. Someone who will set up an IRA, turn you from an individual into a corporation, put you into opportunities. You will never have to open another bill, or write another check, it will all be done for you."

"Great."

"I'm not finished. Someone to track your residuals, invest and hide money if you should move on from Ellen and remarry."

"I'm working on it," Bender said, wondering how Navitz knew so much about his life.

"In that case, you will need to know the difference between separate and community property and learn the art of the prenup. You'd be surprised how many of my clients don't until it is too late."

Bender knew the stories of Hollywood financial wizards who managed the earnings of movie stars, producers, writers, agents, and A-list directors. Some of their clients saw their wealth multiply, others were victims of bad investments, collapsed markets, art forgeries, or simply robbed and forced to declare bankruptcy. The legendary Sol D'Inucci only had six clients, all studio executives. He put them in commercial real estate. The Barish brothers tag-teamed senior ICM agents and put them in natural gas and bull semen (later disallowed by the IRS), the shadowy Nate Vermouth who made his clients sign non-disclosure agreements, then put them into Malaysian hardwood futures. Hank Greenberg put his three movie star clients into an Alberta oil company then moved to Canada. The movie stars never saw Hank or their money again. And of course, the biggest daddy of them all, Bernie Madoff.

"He gets you twelve per cent a year; every year, never less, the man's a genius," Navitz said.

"I'll give him all my money."

"It's not that simple. He's very selective; you need to know somebody who knows somebody who knows him. Guys join his Country Club in Boca Raton just to meet him. Do you have a relationship with Spielberg? He knows him."

"If I had a relationship with Spielberg, I'd give him a screenplay."

"Ha. I'm setting you up with Gary Mosk, he's someone we like very much, we only recommend him to our elite clients."

A week later Bender drove to The Beverly Wilshire for a sit down with Mosk. Was there a conflict of interest in his agent referring him to a business manager? Gary addressed the issue: "I work for you, not Navitz Artists. My loyalty is to you. You sign with me; you become a part of the Mosk family. You understand? You're family. Family is trust. Family is love. Family doesn't fuck each other. You'll come to dinner. Meet my wife, my kids, my mother. You married? No? Bring a date."

A week later, Bender, unable to convince any women he knew, including Ellen, that dinner with an accountant might be fun, drove alone to a cul-de-sac in Brentwood. Mosk hugged him, introduced him to his wife Denise, the twins Derrick and Darren, his mother, Debbie. Denise not only knew his credits; she was a big fan of his first film. Debbie told him how much she liked his second. "I'm a total fan."

The dog wagged its tail.

"See, Bender," Mosk said, "the whole family is one big fan."

Mojitos in hand, Mosk showed Bender his floodlit tennis court, screening room, wine cellar, the private gym. Hockney watercolors lined the walls of the cavernous living room, beige sofas dotted the floor like domes on a pinball game. At dinner Mosk ate three helpings of ribs, drank a bottle of wine, and between courses stepped outside to smoke Nate Shermans.

Bender knew little about investing, but he noted the pallor of Mosk's skin, the beads of sweat dripping down his forehead, his shortness of breath; it was clear this potential manager of his money would not be a prudent long-term investment.

Bender asked Steve for advice.

"Forget all those Hollywood guys. I'm sending you to Siggy Landson. He only does delis and writers. His office looks like shit, he's out of Dickens, but I trust him. Ask Ed Weinberger, he's a client."

Weinberger was rolling in dough. Bender called him.

"I'm thinking of going with Siggy Landson."

"Wise choice. But he makes you write jokes for his birthday parties."

o   o   o

Siggy Landson sat behind a paper-littered desk in his office above an Indian restaurant on Ventura Boulevard. Siggy had a friendly, pudgy face, a smile that said *you can trust me*, essential for a business manager. There was a faint odor in the room of marijuana and corrective air freshener.

Siggy pointed to a chair covered with files. "Just throw that crap on the floor. I always wanted to have an office over a restaurant, like Gene Kelly in *An American in Paris*, have my lunch hoisted up in a basket, but Kishore downstairs got a D from the health department."

As he spoke, Siggy's fingers danced on the keys of a vintage Texas Instruments calculator. "I know, I'm like an Italian male scratching his nuts, they don't itch, he's just making sure they are still there. I'm that way with numbers. Okay, aside from finding you safe, prudent investment opportunities, I have two guiding principles when I work with writers. One, you have to tell me what you need to write; it will be my job to see how I can make that happen. If you write better knowing you have $200,000 dollars in the bank, we will aim for that. If you need a gram of coke and a hooker twice a week, we will make sure you will have the cash for the transactions. I have a client whose name I can't mention who needs a briefcase full of hundreds next to his computer when he begins a screenplay."

It had to be Weinberger.

"What's the other principle?"

Siggy removed his hand from the calculator, stretched his fingers like Horowitz about to play Chopin. "It's not my job to collect taxes for the United States Government. I will do nothing illegal, but your tax liability will be the least amount within the law. It will be my mission to make as much of your life tax deductible."

"How?"

"You are a writer, we will write off your computer, printer, scanner, phones, pencils, movies, clothes, books, newspapers, magazines, home office, car, meals, vacations, hotels, airplanes, even chopped liver if you so desire."

"How do you write off chopped liver?"

"Shirley Denhoff is president of Temple Beth El in Sherman Oaks. She makes the best chopped liver in LA. She gives it to you in return for a nice donation to the Temple, tax deductible, of course."

"This works?"

"I have never lost an audit yet."

Bender nodded, trying to look fiscal but his mind was still on chopped liver.

"Vacations?"

"Easy. Say you fly to Paris for a week. On your tax return, we claim the trip was for research for a screenplay that takes place there. We deduct plane fare, meals, hotels, taxis, you name it. If you want an escort, we write her off as a translator. It's a business expense."

"I'm a big skier."

"No problem, you are writing a comedy about kids who work for the ski patrol. *Bad News Bears* in the snow."

"If I go on a trek in Peru?"

"You'll write about the Aztecs. I like it"

Siggy meant the Incas, but Bender forgave him. "What about Nepal? Kathmandu, maybe see Mount Everest."

"Hey, you're the writer, I'm the accountant. Do I have to do everything?"

There was a handshake.

At the door Siggy said, "February 25th, my birthday. Save the date. We do a big party at The Stinking Rose on La Cienega. All my comedy writers do Siggy jokes."

A few days later Bender gave Siggy power of attorney, his Social Security number, a copy of his California Driver's License, his checkbook, credit card bills and his mother's maiden name. Bender discovered another virtue in handing over his finances to Siggy. He could again feel the comfort of a child's restraints. Faced with a purchase, he had agreed to call Siggy for permission. "I'm looking at a printer; an HP LaserJet, thirty-five hundred bucks."

Bender waited as Siggy fingers danced on the calculator. "Buy it, we'll run it through the corp."

"Siggy, I need a new car. Lease or buy?"

"Just tell me the make, model, color, audio package. I'll get it for you. Landson clients buy, they don't lease. We'll run it through the corp. Just asking, how are my birthday jokes coming?"

o o o

The television executives at Warner Bros. liked Bender's sitcom idea: a failed novelist who gets a job ghostwriting for a deceased author. He churns out novels under her name, they become best sellers, while he can't get anything published under his own.

"They think it's ironic, which is all the rage right now," Navitz said. "You'll write a pilot, then we'll attach one of our top directors."

Bender said, "I'm going skiing at Tahoe next week."

"Good. Ski all day, write all night."

o   o   o

On the last run of the day, Bender found himself alone on the lift line. He called out, "Single!"

A woman in a red ski jacket raised her pole in the air and glided alongside him. Together, they advanced to the lift, boarded a chair, yanked forward up the mountain. A few towers later, the safety bar resting on their knees, the woman removed her helmet and goggles. Bender realized he was sitting next to the most beautiful woman he had ever seen who was not a movie star. He had three or four minutes before they got to the top of the mountain. Should he just introduce himself? *Hi, I'm Bender. Great powder, yes? Have we worked together? Did we meet at the Human Rights Dinner? You must know Neil Navitz.*

Instead, Bender said, "What are you reading these days?"

Her name was Irene, she was a retired fashion model, her answer was *Buddenbrooks*. She said Bender was the first man who had ever asked her that question. They were staying at the same hotel and met up later for an apres-ski swim. Bender posed a question, "When you were a model, did you do that turn, that look, as you come to the end of the runway?"

"Yes.

"Does it have a name?"

"I don't know. But I was good at it."

"Would you do one for me?"

"Here?"

"Yes."

Irene rose out of her lounge chair, walked to the end of the pool, turned, and stood to her full height. She loosened her shoulders like a vaulter ready to sprint to the pole, cocked her hips, sashayed slowly towards Bender, one hand on her waist, came to a stop, inches from his knees. Her crotch was level to his eyes, she stared at him with a mix of contempt and disgust, spun around, and walked away.

Bender applauded. "That was frightening. Do you ever do it to an actual person?"

"Honey, I froze Bono's balls at a Vivienne Westwood show."

During dinner Irene mentioned that she had a French boyfriend. Bender was relieved. Irene was perfect, her perfection frightened him. She had no flaws; life with her would be an endless ordeal of fighting off other men. Leave it to someone else.

"I'm meeting Abhishek in Paris, if you want to come, we could all hang out," Irene said.

Bender knew the Hollywood holiday calendar; a Christmas break that began before Thanksgiving, lasted until the week after New Year's, so everyone could *settle in, get back into the rhythm*. If Bender went to Paris no one would notice. "I could do some research for my next screenplay," he told Siggy.

"Get receipts. We'll deduct, run it through the corp."

Bender checked into the Hotel Luxemburg Parc, scribbled *Research/Paris Screenplay* on his American Express receipt, then walked to La Rotonde, where he met Irene and Abhishek for dinner. Abhishek owned an apartment in the Place des Voges, was a witty sophisticated film lover happily stuck in la nouvelle vague. Bender paid for dinner, wrote *Dinner Meeting with Mossad Agents/Research/Paris Screenplay* on his receipt.

Navitz sent a fruit basket to Bender's hotel with a note that said CBS was close to ordering a pilot but "Don't hurry home, everyone is getting ready for MIFED." The three friends spent a week in Paris, then flew to Marrakech, checked into the Mamounia. Bender wrote *Morocco/Marrakech/Research/Paris Screenplay* on all his receipts, including the camel tour in the Atlas Mountains and the gift shop in the Berber village of Immouzer de Kandar where he bought a blue and gold engraved spice bowl for Ellen, even though she had made it very clear that there were to be no more presents.

o   o   o

Siggy called. His voice had the timbre of a doctor with news of a sour biopsy. "Come to the office, we need to talk. They don't like last year."

"Nobody did. The Lakers went 27 and 55."

"Ha. That's a good one. You should have used it at my birthday party. We have a problem."

A problem? Did Siggy's fingers slip on his calculator, was there a missing signature, a problem with the business losses carried over from the joint interest in the apartment complex in Burbank, or the potato farm in Idaho? Was the IRS disallowing Shirley Denhoff's chopped liver Siggy ran through the corp? H.W. Fowler's Introduction came to him: *I think of it as should have been, with its prolixities docked, its dullness enlivened, its fads eliminated, its truths multiplied.*

"What didn't they like about it? Too prolix?" Bender asked.

"Travel. Aspen."

"That was research for my ski screenplay. I was scouting locations."

"They want to see the screenplay."

"You're kidding me."

"I wish."

"Tell them I'm not finished."

"I had an informal chat with the IRS agent, if you can't show her a screenplay, she will tear you apart and audit your travel as far back as the statute of limitations allows, including your trip to Rome for your Mussolini project."

"Jesus Christ."

"Also your trek to Nepal, and the Inca Trail to Machu Picchu."

"This is crazy."

"Crazy is not the issue. She wants to see the Aspen screenplay, *Ski Bumz.*"

"It doesn't exist."

"You'd better write it."

"How much time do I have?"

"I got you a postponement. Two weeks."

"I can't write a screenplay in two weeks. I'm slow. I take months. Besides, I'm writing one now."

"What's it about?"

"It's an historical drama."

"Can you shift it to Aspen?"

"It takes place in Egypt in 400 BC."

"What's the story?"

Bender took a deep breath, exhaled the plot: "Pompey, a Roman general pursued by Caesar, sails to Egypt. He anchors his fleet off Alexandria. He asks the young King Ptolemy for sanctuary. His ministers debate what to do: if they allow Pompey to come ashore Caesar might punish them, if they don't, there is the danger that Pompey will land with his army and dislodge the King. They decide to invite Pompey ashore for a banquet. As he steps out of his boat, Egyptian soldiers attack and kill him. Days later, Caesar arrives, the Egyptians present him with Pompey's head. Caesar is furious. He says, 'Only a Roman can kill a Roman' and slaughters everyone but Cleopatra."

"Great story," Siggy said.

"It's from Suetonius."

"It might be a stretch to move it to Aspen."

"No shit."

"You must have something in your trunk."

Bender reviewed his inventory of unsold scripts: a sci-fi version of *Heart of Darkness*, the Don Drysdale biopic, a screenplay about an art forger in Key West. None of them could be set in the deep powder of Colorado. He remembered *Lulu*, an abandoned script about a female assassin. Bender could shift it from Washington to Aspen. Instead of Lulu's cover as a sailing instructor in Annapolis, she would teach skiing, give private lessons in winter, and kill bad guys off-season. Forget the gun battles on opposing yachts, instead he'd write chases on skis, red blood on the snow. Bender could make it sexy, too. It wouldn't be *Ski Bumz*, but it would be a screenplay.

"I might have something. But it's a thriller."

"Thriller-schmiller. As long as there's stuff on skis and it takes place in Aspen."

"It's a lot of work. I might have to bail on your birthday party."

"No worries. Look on the bright side. You write the screenplay, maybe you can sell it. Do you need me to get you pills?"

Before he began the rewrite, Bender dialed Weinberger.

"You heard the news?" Weinberger said. "Our dealer's sick."

Bender said. "Jesus, I'm sorry. We're supposed to have lunch next week."

There was a silence, a comedy writer's silence; Weinberger was searching for something funny, but nothing was coming.

"So what's up?" Weinberger finally said.

"Do you have a script about skiing in your trunk?"

"Oh, shit, you're getting audited."

BEVERLY HILLS

Sitting across from Jimmy, Bender dipped a piece of La Scala's *focaccia* into a bowl of olive oil the color of Jimmy's chemo complexion.

"I'm going to beat this," he said. Three weeks later Jimmy was dead.

There was a question as to where to hold the memorial service. Jimmy owned a small ranch in Ojai where he ran an antiques store that served as a money-laundering device for his drug business. Annette, Jimmy's wife, lived on Coldwater Drive behind the Beverly Hills Hotel. She was a four-star estate agent at Coldwell Banker who only sold properties north of Sunset. Annette hated Ojai, Jimmy's dogs, his pet snakes, the junk he called antiques, so the memorial was held in her backyard facing the swimming pool. It was easier for his Los Angeles friends and former customers, most of whom had stopped using the cocaine Jimmy sold. Eventually, there were too many stupid deaths, ruined careers, expensive rehabs, and powder-fueled over-budget films. Personal trainers, yoga, Pilates, juice bars, the obsession for getting children into the best private schools took over. It simply wasn't cool to do coke anymore. Marijuana stayed socially acceptable; and Jimmy was the go-to weed dealer. Jimmy roamed the halls of Hollywood studios peddling pot like Willy Loman. A referral was needed to engage Jimmy. Bender got one from Andre, the bartender at Ports; he called Jimmy.

"Do you need a drive-on pass to get on the Warner lot?" Bender asked Jimmy.

"Not necessary. The guards know me."

The next day Jimmy arrived at Bender's office. He was lanky tall, a full head of brown hair combed straight back like Pat Riley, Ray-Bans perched on a fine aquiline nose and perfect white teeth that may not have been his own. He had a soft surfer's drawl, wore faded jeans, cowboy boots, a linen shirt under a striped Baja hoodie with a loosely tied belt. To Bender, Jimmy looked like what he was: a drug dealer. Her offered to send him right down to TV casting but Jimmy had no use for show business. "Don't take this personally, but you people are all full of shit."

Jimmy opened his leather attaché case. Inside were rows of coded white business envelopes. He handed Bender a sheet of paper with faux Crumb drawings of marijuana plants and a list of prices. "Here's a menu. I deal in eighths, quarters, and kilos, usually for recording studios." Bender looked at the page: Thai, Venom, Luke Skywalker, Kryptonite, Humboldt, Maui. Like his relationship to wine, automobiles, and marijuana, Bender was merely a consumer, ignorant of vintages, spark plugs, the difference between *sativa* and *indica*. At the same time, he didn't want to appear ill informed about a drug he had used since high school. "I have knee pain. Do you have anything for that?" Bender said.

Jimmy handed Bender an envelope. "Bolinas Bold. Anything else?"

"I'm a writer."

Jimmy selected another envelope. "I have Oscar winners who swear by this."

On his way home, Bender stopped at Steve's delicatessen, traded some of his newly purchased weed for a brisket on rye. "This is for pain, and this is for writing," Bender said.

At home, Bender did what he always did with drugs, he locked the marijuana in his stash box along with his pipes, grinders, rolling papers and a diamond hard piece of hash that he had not touched for ten years. He called Steve. "Did you try it?"

"Yeah."

"How was it?"

"My headache's gone, and I can't stop writing."

o   o   o

Most of the mourners in Annette's house were Jimmy's former clients, sober for years, graduates of portfolio-emptying rehab clinics in Malibu, happy to be alive, unlike the ones who didn't stop coke and died in car crashes or lost their careers. Bender recognized people from the film business, but the rest were strangers, probably Annette's real estate colleagues. He nodded to a woman he knew, a loan officer at a Bank of America branch in Westwood who sold ecstasy out of her office. A bank guard escorted Bender to the elevator, then another guard to her third-floor office where he purchased the pills. When Bender worked on a dramatic series he had his own trailer on location. He would leave his stash in his briefcase, step outside where an off-duty LAPD motorcycle policeman was waiting. "No need to lock your trailer, sir. I'll keep an eye on it." Bender marveled at life in Los Angeles where a banker sold him drugs and a cop guarded them.

Annette, mixing with mourners, was in a white blouse, leather jacket, black miniskirt.

"The food is delicious," Bender said.

"I use Lenore from Celebration Concepts. She does all my open houses. Can you stay? I want to talk to you later."

"Sure."

Dale Roth, who wrote action screenplays for Van Damme that didn't get made, was also an ordained minister in the Universal Life Church and conducted the memorial service. He kept it simple, talked about what a good guy Jimmy was (nods)… how much he loved Annette (nods)… how he was responsible for providing joy and spiritual awakening to a lot of people (laughter)… at some risk to himself (nods). Roth said that not many people knew Jimmy loved poetry, then read his favorite poem by Wallace Stevens about blackbirds. Bender was struck by one stanza: *I was of three minds / Like a tree / In which there are three blackbirds.*

Annette handed out lyrics to Jimmy's favorite songs. Accompanied by a waiter on electric piano they sang "All You Need Is Love," "Born to Run," and "Pretty Woman" in honor of Annette. Roth asked if anyone else wanted to speak. There was a shuffled silence that went on too long. Bender caught Annette's pleading look and stepped forward.

"We were all fortunate to have Jimmy in our lives. Jimmy was a businessman, he felt a responsibility to his customers, he always acted in good faith, his product was always first rate, or he gave you your money back." Bender cocked his ear, "What's that, Jimmy? No way." During the laughter, Bender paused on his own silent memory: when Jimmy, after an expensive dinner at Original Joe's in North Beach, reached under his car seat and pulled out a softball size mound of flake coke.

"You have to try this," Jimmy said, slicing off a wedge the size of his thumb, wrapping it in a piece of paper and handing it to Bender. What a pal. What a fucking generous loving pal. A month later Jimmy reminded him that he was owed $1,800 dollars. Bender, too much of a gentleman, wallowing in sitcom money, paid.

"Where was I?"

"Generosity," Roth prompted.

"Thank you. There is a saying in the Talmud: A man will be measured by his friends." Bender had invented this, but who was going to check? "Looking at this gathering, I can say that in the friendship department Jimmy measured way up there. I extend those wise words to include his love for Annette. I write romance for a living, and I can tell you I couldn't write a better one than theirs." Bender had no idea where he was going but it had a good feel, so he continued, "When people find each other as adults they often tend to be skeptical, jaded, cynical. Who can blame them? They've seen too much, been hurt too much, disappointed too many times. It's called baggage. But when Jimmy and Annette fell in love, they left their suitcases in the car. They made it look easy." Bender raised his margarita glass. "Here's to Annette. Here's to Jimmy. Here's to love. Jimmy, we'll miss you."

Annette wiped away a tear and winked at him.

o   o   o

Bender stayed in the kitchen watching the caterers pack up. Annette came in, poured vodkas.

"That was so sweet what you said about us."

"I meant every word."

They picked at a plate of leftover crab cakes.

"Did you know we met at AA? He wanted to take me to Maui, but I told him I wanted to go slow, get to know him first. The truth is I was under house arrest and wearing an ankle bracelet. He told me he was a doctor. Two bullshitters. It was very romantic."

"I didn't know about the ankle bracelet."

"A mess. I was hanging with the wrong people, did some favors, the next thing you know, boom."

"I know only too well." No, I don't, Bender thought. I have no idea what she's talking about. Boom?

They moved on to the cold mini pizzas.

"You want me to put these in the microwave?"

"I'm okay. What are you going to do with Ojai?"

"Jimmy's got a daughter in Tahoe. She can have it."

"Is there…"

"A safe full of money? I wish. He didn't have medical insurance, mine was worth shit. City of Hope took every-thing."

She handed him a worn leather address book. "He left this."

Bender opened the book; there were pages of unintelli-gible names and phone numbers. He looked under the Bs. His name wasn't there. Or maybe it was. It was all coded.

"I assume it's his customers' names," she said.

"So?"

"You're a smart creative guy. You do crosswords, Scrabble. Crack the code and we're in business."

"Isn't the business over? Who does blow anymore? Weed is getting so legal they'll be selling it at Walmart."

"Let's go upstairs, Bender."

o   o   o

On the bed facing the flat screen Sony, Annette informed Bender that the Beverly Hills real estate business still ran on white powder, and if he thought Silicon Valley was all frisbee, salad bars, and yoga, he should grow up. What's more, she had gotten a call from a very nice Colombian gentleman who offered his condolences but said she had a week to resume selling or he would be compelled to give Jimmy's clients to another "manager."

"We can't sell if we don't know who his customers are, can we?" Annette said.

Bender was not comfortable with Annette's choice of pronoun but felt it was too soon to pour cold water on her idea or, for that matter, on his growing attraction for her. Was there a decent interval before one hit on the widow of a friend? Jimmy was a dead drug dealer, a capitalist, Bender leaned to socialism, and Annette was sending obvious signals. A decent interval at the most would be another five minutes.

"Let me see the book again," Bender said, joining her on the bed.

Bender turned to the B page. He had researched codes for an espionage screenplay. Jimmy was using a Caesar Cipher. Substitute one letter for another, shift the alphabet back three places; Y becomes B. YBKABO was BENDER. The phone numbers were even simpler. Jimmy used letters for numbers, so his phone number 592-1808 was EIB AHOH.

Bender figured Jimmy must have gotten the code from a comic book.

"It's a lot of work, but I might be able to figure it out."

"Very cool."

Annette passed him a pipe for another hit of Jimmy's private reserve marijuana, so lethal that two hits were always one too many. On the bed lying respectably parallel, knees touching, they were a short roll away from each other.

"By the way," Annette said, "Jimmy left something for you."

"You're kidding."

"He said of all his friends who weren't criminals you were the one he felt closest to. You guys had a lot in common."

"I think we do. Or did."

What would his inheritance be: one of Jimmy's cars? The '63 Porsche? The rusting Bentley, sitting on cement blocks? A Rolex? Jimmy collected guns, the antique Colt 45? Annette opened the drawer of a bedside table and opened a jeweled pillbox. There were two shiny black capsules the size of Tylenols. "He said we should take these together when he was gone."

"What is it?"

"I don't know."

"Did he say how long we should wait?"

"For what?"

"Until it's appropriate?"

"Appropriate wasn't in his vocabulary," Annette said.

Bender examined the pills. Was this poison? Did Jimmy mean to kill them? Did he sense a post-memorial betrayal?

"You okay with taking this?"

"Me? I'll try anything twice," Annette said.

"You took them? What happened?"

"We fucked all night."

"Can we take it with vodka?"

o   o   o

Bender wasn't sure he was awake, even as he flailed his arms and legs in the bed like a child making snow angels, hitting no one. Where was Ellen, his wife, no, she wasn't his wife anymore, they were divorced. Whose bed was he in? Was he still in a dream? He saw Annette on the floor, curled naked under the makeup table, snoring. Bender gathered his clothes, tiptoed out of the bedroom, and dressed in the hallway. His watch said five in the afternoon, but this was California summer where the scented sunlight stayed open late. Bender drove his Alfa Romeo down Coldwater trying to remember what happened after he and Annette popped the pills. Did they have sex? Bender had no memory of the act. He felt dizzy, was he still in a dream? Pinch himself, it was a cliché. He needed food. The Polo Lounge was the closest restaurant; he'd get a Cobb Salad and a martini. Bender made a quick U-turn, drove back up Crescent Drive to the Beverly Hills Hotel. Writers who took meetings at the Polo Lounge knew better than to pay for the valet parking. Bender found an empty space on Crescent Drive, followed the garden paths into the back entrance to the hotel.

The maître d' stopped him. "I'm afraid you'll need a tie, sir."

"Really? New policy?"

"No, sir. But don't worry, I can give you one."

At the bar, a borrowed maroon knit tie around his neck, Bender suddenly remembered Annette straddling him, eyes burning, her black hair whipping back and forth across her face, gold chains bouncing on her stiff nipples. He felt his groin aim for the ceiling. The bartender put a coaster on the bar. "What's your pleasure, sir?"

"A gin martini, straight up, olives on the side."

"Coming right up."

Bender closed his eyes trying to recall more of Annette. No use. The bartender poured his martini into a glass. Bender put a bill on the bar and took a sip. He heard the ring of the cash register, the bartender fanned out his change next to the olives: three fives, four ones.

"Bartender? I gave you a twenty."

"Yes, sir."

"You gave me nineteen dollars."

"Yes, sir. Martini's a dollar."

"Wow. Is that a special?"

"Raised the price last week. Guess there wasn't enough profit in charging seventy-five cents."

Bender gripped the bar, was he already tipsy? The Polo Lounge was filling up. The maître d' greeted regulars, led them to prized booths where waiters were already setting down their drinks. The women wore dresses, the men in suits. He hadn't been here in months, but this was obviously a new dress code. Where were the black t-shirts, the torn jeans? He fingered his tie. Who wore knit ties anymore? A short middle-aged man in a double-breasted suit sat down on a stool next to him. He took out a pack of Lucky Strike, tapped one out and caught Bender staring at him.

"Sorry, would you like one?"

"You're not allowed to smoke in here," he said. "Not that I care much myself."

"Who says?"

"Who says what?"

"Who says I can't smoke?"

"It's the law. You can't smoke indoors. It's illegal."

"Bullshit."

The man flicked a gold Ronson lighter. The bartender brought the man his drink and pushed an ashtray next to the glass. "Peanuts, gents?"

At the other end of the bar, perched on stools were two women in summer flowered dresses. Bender placed them as working girls, in for the cocktail hour, available for a drink, dinner, and then sex in a studio-paid-for bungalow or a room already booked. One stole a quick look at Bender over her friend's shoulder, whispered to the other, who had her back to him. The friend turned, reached for her purse but Bender, a practiced observer of observations, knew she was checking him out on the instructions of the other woman. They were different ages, the younger one might be an actress, the older teaching her how to work hotels, introducing her to bartenders, bellhops, concierges, all the links in the chain of high-end prostitution. The younger one smiled into the bar mirror, flashed a row of white teeth, dimples creased in each cheek, and now, with a full view of her face, Bender realized if the camera didn't love her, it had no taste. He smiled back at her in the mirror. A call girl that gorgeous? It was possible. This was Hollywood, the destination for the beautiful. Shopgirls at Robinson's had been beauty queens in their hometowns. It was more than possible. At one point, deep in his own depths of divorce misery, a producer slipped Bender a phone number.

"Take a break, kid," he said. "She's a lot of fun, specializes in writers."

Duly depressed, Bender dialed, reached an answering service, left his number and the first name of the producer.

An hour later a woman called. Bender realized if he wrote her speech there would be no commas.

"Hi this Sandy George said you were cute."

"He said you were, too."

"I can see you tonight if you want where do you live I hope not in the Valley I hate the Valley please say the West Side."

"Benedict Canyon."

"Thank god I'm calling a cab what's your address I get a hundred and fifty."

As Bender showered, remade his bed, put some white wine in an ice bucket, he realized he was getting ready for an encounter with a woman that had a guaranteed conclusion. Who would arrive at his door? Sadie Thompson, Nana, Elizabeth Taylor from Butterfield 8? A Pigalle *poule* in a slit skirt, dangling a Gauloise in red lips, like the one student tourist Bender had glimpsed from a bus window in Paris. The doorbell rang, a woman in a Lakers cap, Giorgio's t-shirt, and a denim mini, hopped on one foot.

"Honey pay the cab I gotta use the bathroom."

When Bender returned, he found her in the living room. "I love your art you're too sexy so let's hit the bedroom then talk."

Bender, who had never made love with a stranger, or been made love to by one, was told a few minutes later, "Honey I want the name of your trainer you relax and let me do my thing."

Bender found himself simultaneously flattered and lied to, with images of Ellen shaking her head at his depravity, factors which he blamed for his inability to perform.

"That's okay honey we can just talk if you want."

Bender was already paying Dr. Grotstein for talking. Pay for two conversations? Sex for money was no answer for him, he would have to suffer depression for free. It was a dead end, he'd end up like Herman Leon, a paunchy high-priced joke genius who wrote for late-night shows and only saw expensive call girls. Herman bragged that he had slept with more beautiful women than Warren Beatty. Herman asked his favorite, Alma, a former Miss Arkansas, if she would come to his funeral when he died. Alma said, "If you paid me."

At the bar, Bender took another sip of his martini and inhaled the rich smoke of his neighbor's Lucky Strike. His head spun. There was something very wrong in this Polo Lounge. Bender slid off his stool and walked over to the two women at the end of the bar. The older woman nudged her young companion.

"I can buy both of you a drink, but you already have one. They don't sell flowers, so I have no excuse to talk to you other than I would never forgive myself if I didn't."

Not very good, but it got tiny laughs from both. The older woman had a few thin lines under her makeup, a bright red mouth he wanted to kiss, folds of flesh squeezing the straps of her dress. Bender leaned in between the women, placed his drink on the bar and whispered to the older one.

"If I cut to the chase and asked you how much, what would you say?" Like a ventriloquist with frozen lips, Bender heard the words but didn't see her say them.

"Twenty-five."

Case closed. The knit tie, Lucky Strikes, a dollar martini, and no woman that beautiful at the Polo Lounge Bar charged twenty-five dollars for sex. It was obvious. "Does anyone know the date?"

The young one perked up. "August something."

"It's the fifth," the older one said.

"And the year?"

The two women looked at each other. Who doesn't know the year? The young one giggled, "Nineteen thirty-nine."

Bender knew what Jimmy's pill did. It had put him in a dream he couldn't exit; he had swallowed a pharmaceutical time machine.

"Will you excuse me?"

Bender headed for the door, caught a glance of the bartender sweeping his nineteen dollars into his tip jar. Outside, under the dull green avocado trees that lined the paths to the tennis courts, Bender threw up into a rose bush. A bellhop pushing a luggage cart stopped. Bender waved him away.

"I'm okay, thanks."

He headed east to the sidewalk on Crescent Drive. The parked cars appeared to be placed by a production designer with an unlimited budget, massive Buicks, Cadillacs, Hudsons, a Cord, a Packard, and a Nash Suburban with wooden side panels. He couldn't see his Alfa; it didn't exist yet. This was getting complicated. If he couldn't wake up or get out of this time-travel box, he would have to find a way to survive in 1939 Hollywood.

It came to Bender quickly: write movies that hadn't been made yet, find an agent, pitch *Star Wars, E.T., Easy Rider, The Godfather;* he knew the Beatles catalogue, he'd plunk out "All You Need is Love," "I Want to Hold Your Hand," and "Hey Jude" on a piano, make millions. It was too soon for Microsoft, but there was IBM, and TWA. Rich and famous, he'd have a regular booth at Chasen's, drink with Bogart, Bacall, Trumbo. He wouldn't sign petitions, avoid Reds later in the fifties; date movie stars, buy land in the San Fernando Valley. World War II was coming. So what? He would enlist in the Signal Corps, write training films for George Stevens, and volunteer at the Stage Door Canteen, maybe talk Ronald Reagan out of a career in politics, or at least get him to turn down General Electric Theater.

Bender's future in the past stretched out before him. He had written one unsold screenplay about time travel and did an uncredited rewrite on another. He knew the pitfalls, he wouldn't marry his future mother (or was it his grandmother?) or try to kill Hitler or change history, he'd eat sensibly, avoid saturated fats and sugar. What about his parents? They planned to see each other over Christmas. But he wasn't born yet. Dizzy, Bender sat down on the grass. This was fucked. None of those movies could be made. *Star Wars*? Science fiction in 1939 was Buster Crabbe as Flash Gordon; a special effect was a model spaceship hung with fishing line. A movie about two stoned guys on motorcycles? He would be tossed out on his ass at Disney. Persuade Katharine Hepburn to fake an orgasm in a deliacatessen? The Beatles? Bender envisioned auditioning 'Let It Be' to a music publisher who would sell it for The Andrews Sisters, or 'Eleanor Rigby' going to Roy Rogers. Fucked.

"You okay, honey?"

It was the young woman from the bar.

Bender crossed his legs in front of him in a lotus pose. "I was meditating."

She plunked down next to him. "You forgot your wallet."

"Thanks. That's very nice of you."

"You look kind of pale."

Bender looked at her. Was it possible? "What's your name?"

"Norma."

"Norma Jean?"

"How did you know?"

Oh, it was more than possible, it was true. The future was sitting beside him on the grass in front of the palm-shrouded bungalows of The Beverly Hills Hotel, holding his hand. Her voice was the familiar warm whisper, Bender felt a stirring, something was pulling at him, taking him out of this time. Bender had only a few moments more; he was leaving the past. This would be Bender's chance to change history. "Listen to me," he said," I want to give you some advice. No, it's more than advice. It's an order. You must take what I am about to say very seriously."

"Sure. Shoot."

"Walk away from your friend and the life she is leading you into. You must go to acting school, get pictures, go to auditions. You will be a movie star. A huge movie star, I promise."

"Really?"

"I'm a screenwriter, I've seen hundreds of actresses. I know what I'm talking about. You have it, you will make it."

Bender stood up, took her hands in his, stared into the face that launched a thousand fantasies. His heart bounced and bumped and settled. He rehearsed his last words to her: Norma Jean, I have to go now. Too much, cut Norma Jean.

"I have to go now," Bender said.

"Why?"

"My work is done."

She moved closer, Bender smelled lilacs, he felt her breasts against his chest, please let me remember this, he thought, Norma Jean put her arm around his neck, kissed him on the lips and lingered long enough so that he would remember.

"What's your name?"

"Bender."

"You're a good kisser, Bender."

o   o   o

"You okay?" Annette was sitting on the edge of the bed. "Did you have a bad dream?"

Bender looked around the room. Flat screen Sony, check, Stairmaster in the corner, check, a bottle of Diet Coke on the night table, check. He was awake, he was in the present. It was a dream.

"That was some pill," he said.

"No kidding."

"Did you dream?"

"I think so. But I never remember them, did you?"

Bender was about to tell her, then changed his mind. "Did you know a martini in the Polo Lounge in 1939 only cost a dollar."

"That sounds high," Annette said.

"It's true."

"Why did this come up?"

"I was just thinking about what an exciting place it must have been then. Sitting at the bar, chatting with Bogart, Bacall, Irwin Cooper, Marilyn Monroe."

"Not Monroe."

"Why?"

"They wouldn't have let her in."

"Huh?"

"I'm a Monroe freak. I know every detail of her life. She was born in 1926, so she would have been thirteen in 1939. The restaurant yes, but not the bar."

"Thirteen? Marilyn Monroe aka Norma Jean…"

"Mortenson."

"Thirteen years old?"

"Do the math."

Bender never did the math. He had an aversion to precision, detail, and conclusions based on data. Feeling it was right was good enough. Let mathematicians, budgeters, accountants have their day; he based his arguments on generosity, charity, and fairness. Bender knew he couldn't take over Jimmy's business. He would be a failure, a victim to undercover narcs, allow rivals to infringe on his territory, he couldn't use a scale if his life depended on it. Bender was condemned to a life of imagination. "Annette, about Jimmy's book? I could never crack that code. I can't do it."

"Too bad. If you could, you'd never have to write again."

Never have to write again? He'd rather drive off a Mulholland cliff.

At the door, Annette said, "I'm sorry, I said a dumb thing. I sell real estate, I hate it. I'd rather sell coke. I didn't mean that you should feel the same way about writing."

"It's okay. Sometimes I feel like I'd rather sell real estate."

"You made a nice speech."

"Thanks. Are there any more black pills?"

"I doubt it, but I'll look the next time I'm in Ojai."

If Annette did find more pills, would Bender take one, then go back in time, and stay in New York with Ellen. Should he change his own history? On Crescent Drive, the palm trees whispered no.

BURBANK

Bender's monthly check-in lunch with Neil Navitz now took place in the executive dining room at Warner Bros. As they ate, the uber-agent glanced over Bender's shoulder, eyes darting from table to table, landing on stars, producers, executives, and directors. Contact made, Navitz silently shook his head, nodded, shrugged, winked, raised a finger from his fork, pointed with a knife, communicating in his own sign language: *"I'll call you after lunch." "Wait for me, I'll stop by your table." "I read the script; no way I'm giving it to Costner." "I don't know who you are so don't approach me." "Sigourney is still reading."*

At the same time, Navitz stayed focused on Bender. He gave him his full attention; laid out his plans for Bender's future while picking at a chopped vegetable salad no dressing.

"I know you want to be in film. Why is not my business as there is much more money in television but I can move you from one to the other. I'm sending you a screenplay this afternoon. Paramount bought it. It's a piece of shit but it has a chance to get a green light because Dustin has already expressed a tentative maybe. There is also a part for his daughter's boyfriend. I will get you the rewrite. You have the voice for this, if the movie is made you will immediately move up on the credibility ladder."

Piece of shit? Bender envisioned Yeats handing Eliot's *The Waste Land* to Ezra Pound. "Ez, it's a piece of shit, but if you whip it into shape, cut and paste, there's a chance I can get it into *The Dial*. Tom will owe you big time. He's on the short list to edit *The Transatlantic Review*." Bender was imagining a literary ballet danced on half-truths so he put an end to it before Navitz could notice he was daydreaming.

"This is amazing, Neil. I'll read it right away."

"You're a good writer, I wouldn't represent you if you weren't, but you also believed in me, you were one of the first clients to come with me to NAA. I will work my ass off to take you to the top."

Lunch was over. There was no check. Long ago Navitz had arranged for every trendy restaurant, deli, omakase sushi bar, including, it was rumored, the Culver City In-N-Out, not to present him with a check, but instead have it sent to his office in Century City. Bender knew the 'end of lunch' protocol; a quick embrace, mutual back-pats, then walk away, allowing Navitz to deliver on his gestured promises.

On the way to his office, Bender tried to come up with an excuse to drop into B-331 in the Producers Building, where Mimi, in between her novel and screenplay rewrites had a job as Rocky Crane's development executive. Her AA sponsor, a twice Oscar-nominated director, advised her to get a day job, do her writing on weekends. "Your days will be full, your writing time more precious, there are noon AA meetings on the lot." One rainy afternoon, Mimi and

Bender were sitting on Rocky's couch. Mimi was crying, she had just broken up with Paul, "For the last time, I swear."

Bender handed her a Kleenex, "I think I'm finally ready to move on."

Mimi told him that she wasn't looking for anything permanent; she needed nights to concentrate on her writing. But she was open to an occasional dinner and *see what happens*, just not on Rocky's couch with Bogart and Bacall looking down from a framed poster of *To Have and Have Not*.

Rocky Crane had a first-look producing deal at Warner's that gave him an office, a fat expense account, with a salary for Mimi. Everyone knew Rocky got the deal because he was Jack's best friend. His mission was to find a starring role for Jack then attach himself as producer. Rocky took pitches from writers, while Mimi answered Rocky's phone, read spec screenplays, galleys of novels, clipped magazine articles, anything that might interest Jack. Rocky sent them on to Jack, but screenplays, treatments, synopses, and articles piled up on his nightstand unread. Rocky teased the studio with reports that Jack was circling something, but the reality was Jack was tired of acting. He was wealthy, the idea of months in a foreign hotel, spending days doing a stupid motorcycle chase gave him an anxiety attack. He only wanted to devote his remaining time on earth to his buffalo ranch in Wyoming, fly to Los Angeles for Lakers games, or make sculpture out of coat hangers. If Jack announced his retirement the studio would cancel Rocky's deal, Mimi would have to get another job, and Bender would lose his best friend on the lot.

Rocky was depressed, his studio days were numbered, he only came to the office to make calls that were increasingly unreturned. He let everybody know he had to leave early to get ready for a Laker game as Jack's courtside guest.

Bender entered Rocky's office suite.

"Look who's here," Mimi said.

Bender peered past her into Rocky's office; his eyes landed on the couch.

"Forget it, he's on his way back."

"I stopped by to ask you if you want to have dinner tonight."

"Hmm. That might be nice."

Bender heard wheels turning as she calculated the factors that determined a Los Angeles encounter: miles, traffic, and a car's age.

"I have a six o'clock shrink in Santa Monica."

Bender countered, "How about Beverly Glen? Fabrocinni's at eight?"

"OK, I'll come to your house after my shrink. It's silly to take two cars."

o   o   o

Every day, Bender awoke at seven, drove to UCLA, and jogged sixteen laps on the Drake Track. Every day except Sunday. No matter what. No matter who.

"Where are you going?"

"Jogging. Want to come?"

"What about cuddling, coffee?"

"I'll be back in one hour. I'll stop at Peete's on the way home. Give me your order, go back to sleep."

Bender came to recognize the regulars on the track: a pair of middle-aged women walking briskly, always in conversation, Burt Lancaster in sweats who wore a towel around his neck, a trio of men who argued politics, and a lean, tanned man in his sixties with a pigeon-toed step. He carried a vial of pills in his left hand, a stopwatch in his right. Bender wrote the man's biography: a retired widowed New York clothing manufacturer, who lived with his daughter and son-in-law in Brentwood. He joined Hillcrest Country Club for golf, Temple Israel for the High Holy Days, Hollywood Park for the races. He took his grandchildren to Dodger games, Disneyland, with an eye out for the next opportunity. One morning Bender found himself jogging alongside him. They small-talked their way into who they were and where they stood in the world. He had gotten everything wrong about the jogger except Hillcrest Country Club. Julie Epstein owned an Oscar for writing *Casablanca*; he was also the only one who got a nod from Burt.

Julie and Bender became jogging partners; they owned the same pace and talked comfortably. Julie entertained him with stories about his years as a contract writer at Warner Bros.

"You want to know what it was like then? Okay. Saturday night at Chasen's with a date; cocktails, Caesar salad, filet mignon, Baked Alaska. The bill was twelve bucks. I was making five thousand dollars a week. That's what it was like." Julie had no nostalgia. "Most of the movies we made were crap. You couldn't put a married couple in the same bed. All those so-called colorful studio executives, they were fucking racist idiots. They hated unions, and considered writers less than dog shit, no thank you. We weren't making art. We were making a living. Movies in those days were prevented from reality. Every leading man had to be a great sexual athlete. Every boy and girl had to 'meet cute,' and the girl had to dislike the hero when they met. If a woman committed adultery, she had to die. And there's no Easter Bunny, either. By the way, Bender, how's your love life these days? Still mooning over Ellen?"

"She's on my mind. I hope I'm on hers."

"You'll get over her, or maybe not. I'm still upset about Elizabeth Taylor but that's another story. Come for dinner, forget about women, concentrate on your writing. You could use a home-cooked meal, I can tell. We eat early, trays in front of six-thirty CBS News. Friday, we do a *faux shabos*, we light candles but don't expect kosher."

Julie's wife Ann wore flannel slacks and white blouses with soft cashmere sweaters. Her pageboy cut framed a softly sculpted unlined face. Moving gracefully to Sinatra CDs she cooked fat-free meals of grilled chicken, steamed vegetables, chopped salad with lemon juice. Julie would live forever. After dinner Julie took Bender to the patio, with a grand view of the Bel-Air Golf Club. Julie smoked a cigar, they listened to Los Angeles night music; angry birds, escaped parrots, the howls of hungry coyotes.

"Once in a while a deer shows up and eats Ann's roses. It's a lot of nature for a Brooklyn boy."

Ann invited him for Thanksgiving, then Christmas. There was a tie from Carroll's for Bender under the tree.

Julie said, "The grandkids want a Christmas tree. For us it's Hanukah, so we put a *dreidel* on top. You'll come to our New Year's cocktail party. "

Ann said, "We send you home at ten, you can watch the ball drop in your own house."

o   o   o

In Fabrocinni's Bender and Mimi shared *Insalate Frutti di Mare, porcini risotto per due, branzino,* and *tiramisu.* Mimi had San Pellegrino and Bender drank a half bottle of Chianti.

A thick Navitz Artists envelope lay propped against Bender's front door. In the living room Mimi wriggled out of her shoes, stretched out next to him on the couch. She put her feet on his lap. "Sorry, Bender, I have to pass out."

Bender opened the envelope. There was a handwritten note from Navitz stapled to a screenplay: "Call me when you read this no matter what time."

The screenplay was *Twins* by Julius J. Epstein.

Twin One, a gentle naïf, is in a mental asylum, Twin Two, a narcissist bully runs a movie studio. A plot twist has them switching places, so Twin One poses as his brother, while Twin Two gets crazier and crazier. It was a comedy that could attract a star to play both brothers. Whatever it was, it wasn't a piece of shit. But he couldn't figure out what was wrong with it. He dropped the script on the floor. It was four o'clock in the morning, his brain was numb. Wriggling out from under Mimi's legs, he weaved his way to the bathroom, bent over the toilet and sent back his Italian dinner.

The next morning Navitz called. "I'm setting up a meeting with Lynda Graves at Paramount. I like her a lot. Give her your take; she'll give you hers. I'll talk to business affairs in the meantime."

"Actually, it's not so bad."

"What is?"

"The screenplay."

"No, it's bad. It needs a page one rewrite." Bender heard the annoyance in Navitz's voice.

"Who says it does?" Bender said.

"Who says? The studio, the director, the star I'm putting in it."

"Why don't they ask Julie to do it?"

"Who's Julie?"

"Julie Epstein. He wrote it. Why don't they ask him to rewrite it?"

"Because they bought it. You buy a screenplay you bring in a new writer."

"Why did they buy it?"

"They bought it because they liked it, now that they own it, they don't like it, so they are hiring you to make them like it again. When you have turned in your draft, they will probably not like it again, they will hire another writer to write until there is a draft they will like. It's not personal, if the movie gets made, I will make sure you get the credit no matter what the Writers Guild says. You will be perceived by the community as the writer."

"I'm having doubts about doing it. Julie's a friend." He heard his own voice, it was thin, a coward's protest, it was another betrayal hatching.

There was a pause. "I'll call you back. I have Mike Nichols on hold."

Bender felt the signs of depression, his markers of despair: he didn't take his mother's call, sent Bari to Fat Burger for a second lunch, and donated money to a Maine Congresswoman.

He called Mimi. "I feel like shit."

"You have to do yoga," she said.

"Now?"

"Yes, Rocky's out. Come right over."

Bender helped push back her desk. He looked at Rocky's couch. Mimi shook her head. "I said yoga."

"Okay."

"Follow me. Feet together, fold your hands under your chin. As you breathe in for a count of six, bring your arms up and then slowly exhale for a count of six as you bring your hands down."

Bender followed her directions. "Now what?"

"We'll do it three more times."

"Can't I take a nap on Rocky's couch?"

"No."

Mimi's phone rang. "It's Rocky's private line. I have to take it."

Bender exhaled; Mimi listened, then passed him the phone. "It's Navitz."

"I knew I'd find you there. Don't talk, just listen," he said. "I can get you out of this. I don't like unhappy clients. But the problem is that it will leave bad memories in certain quarters. I fought to get you a more than unreasonable price, I will now appear weak. Have you read Sun Tzu's *The Art of War*?"

It was Navitz's Bible, his navigational guide to Hollywood. Bender had read it, but as far as he could figure, it would only come in handy if he had to lead an army against Chiang Kai-shek. "You gave me a copy when I signed with the agency."

"Then you will remember what Sun Tzu says, *'Victorious warriors win first and then go to war, while defeated warriors go to war first and then seek to win.'* You are two produced screenplays away from telling me to go fuck myself. Do the job or look for a new agent."

Bender nodded. Navitz heard his nod. "Good. I'm setting up a meeting at Paramount with Linda Graves. Give her your take on the script."

The next morning, Bender jogged silently next to Julie.

"You're quiet today, kid. Still hung up on your ex?"

"No. Just work stuff."

"Let me tell you it doesn't go away. I haven't heard from my agent about my screenplay. In my day when you turned in a script Jack Warner called the next day. He either fired you or shooting started in a month. You know what? I predict the bastards are going to replace me. Probably with some fucking TV hack."

o   o   o

"I know what's wrong with it," Mimi said.

"Tell me."

"Julie writes about the bad twin, the studio executive, but it's out of date. That guy doesn't exist anymore. It's set in the present, but Julie's stuck in the past. Studio executives don't drive Rolls-Royces, they drive Hondas. They don't drink martinis at lunch, or care if nobody knows who John Ford is. They don't know who John Ford is either."

He knew he could fix all of that in five minutes. "What else?"

"It's too tame. There are no dick jokes, no fart jokes, no performance anxiety, everybody's white, the women all talk like Shirley Jones."

At Paramount, Lynda Graves was totally on board with Bender's (Mimi's) take on the screenplay. Her assistant Dulcie took notes, pronounced it brilliant and even evoked Julia Child biting into a slab of *foie gras.* "Um, um, I love your ideas."

Bender was busy elsewhere; up to his knees in guilt as he composed his confession to Julie: *I'm the fucking TV hack they hired to rewrite your screenplay. But I'm going to donate my fee to Temple Isaiah.* Would this lessen his betrayal of Julie, his friend, his mentor? Dr. Grotstein might suggest Oedipal motives. Bender, taking the rewrite job was symbolically killing his father and marrying Ann. Bender's father was a marvelous man; he wanted no other. Dr. Grotstein was bird-watching in the Amazon. Bender pictured Julie, hearing his confession, clutching his chest, falling to his knees, pills spilled on the track, joggers tripping over him. Better to tell him at home, but first he would make sure Ann was in the room so she could call 911.

"Bender?"

"Sorry, Lynda. My head's already into the new draft. I want to get started on this right away. Dulcie, please send me your notes."

As they said good-bye, Bender sensed a remoteness in Lynda. Was she thinking about the next writer, the one to replace Bender, then the writer after that writer, and the writer who would replace that writer until the membership of the Writers Guild was exhausted? Navitz was right. This was the movie business; the re-writes were never ending; it would be Jarndyce v Jarndyce in *Bleak House.*

The elevator arrived, Dulcie, Lynda's assistant, followed Bender. "I'm glad I caught you; I wanted to tell you how much I liked your ideas for the rewrite."

"I look forward to your notes on the next draft," Bender said, hoping he sounded sincere.

"That's what I wanted to tell you. I'm leaving."

"Leaving?"

"I got a job at ABC TV. In comedy."

"Then I'll certainly see you again," Bender said.

"Really?"

"Yes."

"Cool," Dulcie said.

"Cool," Bender agreed.

o   o   o

That night on Julie's terrace the lights of Century City were dulled in fog, the parrots asleep, the coyotes silent, there were no raccoons splashing in the pool. Bender's confession emerged fitfully. "About your screenplay…"

"Good of you to ask, kid, but I still haven't heard a word."

"I was offered the rewrite."

Julie took a long puff on his cigar, then flicked it onto the lawn where it sat glowing red. "You take it?"

"Yes."

There was a whistling noise, followed by the coughs and hisses of the lawn sprinklers dousing the cigar.

"That was my last one. You know, I never really liked cigars."

"Then why do you smoke them?"

"Probably because my father did. I preferred marijuana."

"Really?"

"What, you think you invented it? I hung out with Dexter Gordon and Wardell Gray on Central Avenue. Bobby Mitchum and I were pals."

"Wasn't he arrested for weed?"

"It was a set-up by the LA cops. He was hanging out with friends, one of whom informed on him, they broke into his house, found a couple of muggles. That's what we called it then. Bobby got sixty days. Didn't hurt his career, Howard Hughes loved him, so he spread a lot of money around to make it go away. Bobby used to send his assistant to Rosarita

Beach to bring it back in a golf bag. Now I hear you can buy it in Ralph's in Westwood."

"Not quite. But I have some in my car."

"No, thanks."

They sat in silence. There was the sound of a splash.

"Fucking raccoons are back."

Julie got out of his chair and retrieved the soggy cigar butt. He threw it over the fence into his neighbor's property.

"So? What was wrong with my screenplay?"

"Too tame, out of step with today's raunchiness, too white, too polite."

"I should have known better. I showed it to my agent, Ben Benjamin. He's older than me. He said it was too dirty. Told me to take out the fart jokes, all the stuff about small dicks and big cunts. In my draft, the studio executive was a cross dresser, his wife was always angry at him for stretching her sweaters. She says to him, 'Marvin, you shoulda married someone your own size.'"

"Not bad."

"I took out all the stuff Sam hated, then he took it to Marty Minkoff who has a deal at Paramount. Marty is old school, too, but he gave it to Navitz who took it to Dustin. Nobody ever told me they wanted a rewrite. Fucking Ben, why did I listen to him?"

"Do you have that draft?"

"Of course."

"Could I see it?"

"I'm ahead of you. You turn it in as your rewrite, get the money, it'll go to the Guild for arbitration. You'll lose the arbitration, I'll get sole credit, Navitz will tell everyone you wrote it, but I don't care."

"I'm sorry."

"About what?"
"That I took the job."
"If not you, someone else."
Julie sat back on the chaise.
"It still feels like a betrayal," Bender said.
"Forget it, Bender, it's Hollywood."

HOLLYWOOD

Because his affair with Dulcie Keller turned lethal, Bender asked Navitz for advice. "I'm in trouble, Neil. I've been dating a woman who turns out to have an insanely jealous ex-boyfriend. He's stalking me, threatening to kill me. What should I do?"

"You could start by getting the fuck out of my office."

"Seriously?"

"Just kidding. Have you thought of getting a dog?"

"I have a dog. He wouldn't scare a cat."

"Get a gun."

Bender drove to Retting's Gun Depot on Washington Boulevard. The salesman listened sympathetically. "You'll want something that makes a statement. For stopping power, you can't beat the Smith & Wesson Forty-Four Magnum. But I must warn you, it's an expensive weapon."

"I'd be getting the best, right?"

"It was Clint's choice in *Dirty Harry*. Did you see it?"

"See it? I know the guy who wrote it."

The salesman handed the pistol to him. It weighed a ton.

"How much?" Bender asked.

"This one's used. I can let you have it for $1,500."

"What does that mean, exactly?"

"Just that it's been fired, then traded in. We guarantee it."

"Ah. Broken in."

"Yes."

"Does it come with bullets?"

"I'll throw some in."

Could Bender sound dumber? He tried, "Can you wrap it?"

"Sorry, when you buy a handgun, you need to fill out an application for a background check. It takes about two weeks before you're approved."

"What do I do in the meantime? I'm being threatened."

"I can show you some terrific shotguns, no waiting period."

Bender returned to his car with a $2,000 Benelli Super Black Eagle II semiautomatic shotgun and a box of shells. The salesman advised him to take a course in using the weapon, but Bender had written screenplays with characters who used firearms, so a course wasn't necessary.

Bender's house above Benedict Canyon was two miles from the Polo Lounge. Visitors admired the view, the quiet, the wildlife. Bender was ambivalent about all three. The view stretched to the Pacific, spectacular during the day, but he was rarely home to see it. The night silence was useful for writing but could turn nightmarish with a soundtrack of death screams of cats and small dogs being torn to shreds by coyotes.

Bender removed the shotgun from its box, read the owners' manual. Signore Giovanni Benelli welcomed him to the Benelli family, Bender was now an owner of the finest shotgun in the world. He opened the box of shells, inserted two into the chamber and pumped it. That was easy. It was loaded, ready to fire. Now what? A test shot across Benedict Canyon into the trees? What if there was a hiker? A troop of girl scouts boiling water for hot chocolate? What about the sound? Would his neighbors call the cops? Bender raised the gun to a bare wall above the fireplace. This was not a television remote; point, select a channel, press play, this was point, pull the trigger then call his handyman Henry to repair a foot-wide hole in the plaster. Did the world's finest shotgun have a safety? Bender flipped the manual pages to the index, found *Sicurezza/Safety.*

Now what? Where to keep the gun? Under his bed? But what if the threatening ex-boyfriend was at the front door while he was in the kitchen? Would he have time to run to the bedroom? In the hall closet? Could he tell guests to put their coats next to the Benelli? Lean it against the wall near the front door? Perhaps the umbrella stand? He didn't have an umbrella stand. Maybe he should have bought two shot-guns, one for the front door, one for under the bed. Better to unload it first. He had no idea; the instruction book was unhelpful. How the fuck did he get into this mess? He knew. Like all his messes, innocently enough. It was a desire for companionship, a yearning for a partner, someone to share popcorn at a movie, rub sunscreen on a bare back, a high five at a Lakers game, and a shortcut to get over Ellen.

Dulcie

Dulcie Keller advanced quickly in comedy administration at ABC, and happily for Bender, succeeded Norman Robbins as creative liaison to Bender's show. Robbins' downfall came after weeks of condescending script comments. Bender listened politely as Norman read his notes.

"I think you need to make act one much funnier," Robbins said.

Funnier? Fuck you.

"And I'd like a stronger motivation for Benny in the second scene."

You'd like? Fuck you.

"And I need a better second act ending."

You need? Fuck you.

"That's it. Send me the new draft ASAP."

Up yours.

"Thanks, Norman. I'll get this to the writers' room immediately."

Bender called Navitz.

"I'll take care of it." Navitz made one call, Norman was transferred to another show and Dulcie was now working with Bender. She had a gentler approach:

"I love the way the show opens."

I had a crush on you in the elevator.

"I almost think this scene is too funny."

I may be in love.

"Can I tell you over dinner after the taping?"

"Sure."

Christine

Looking back, Bender realized Christine Deutsch would not have come into his life if there had been smaller mobile phones. Neil Navitz had one of the earliest versions in Hollywood, a foot-long white Motorola DynaTAC. He traveled to meetings with his Stanford educated assistant whose job was to carry the phone, stay alert for Navitz's instructions, then dial a number and say, "I have NN for you." Initials that made careers soar or crash. Bender did not have an assistant; he used a physician's answering service with live operators who took messages from patients about chest pains, high temperatures, prescriptions, hypochondriacal complaints, and missed appointments. Bender's messages were social. When Bender finally set up voice mail, he called Ace Message Service, collected his latest messages, and terminated his account. A few minutes later there was a call.

"Mr. Bender?"

"Yes."

"It's Christine."

"Christine?"

"Deutsch. From Ace. I take your calls."

He recognized the voice. "Of course. Christine."

"I heard you're leaving the service."

"I am. I did."

"Can I ask why?"

"I'm on voicemail."

"Yeah, everybody is. We'll miss you."

"I will, too." Should he have sent a farewell muffin basket? There was a pause. Bender sensed she wanted something.

"I've been taking your calls for three years. It's funny that I know so much about your life, but we've never met."

"Yes?"

"I'm quitting Ace, too. I'm moving to Phoenix. Could we meet for a drink?"

"Meet?"

"I'd love to see who you are in person, that's all."

"When?" he said.

"How about tonight?"

"I can't. I'm busy."

"You're not. Steve cancelled your dinner at Musso's. I just took the message."

A drink? A woman? An adventure?

"Okay. Where? What time?"

"Eight o'clock. The Wagon Wheel on Alvarado. Do you know it?"

"I do," Bender said, but couldn't remember why.

"Good. It's a date."

"A date?"

"Not a date. It's just an expression."

"Right. An expression."

Dulcie

After the Friday night taping Bender met Dulcie at a Mexican restaurant in a mini mall on Victory Boulevard. He felt her knee bump his under the table while they ate fish tacos with Margaritas so cold his jaw ached. He walked Dulcie to her tiny Mazda convertible. Television scripts littered the passenger seat. He leaned in, they kissed, on their way to more, but even in Hollywood the rule was not on the first date. Dulcie's tongue rolling in Bender's mouth made it clear there would be more than more.

"Dinner Friday?"

"Yes."

"The Palm?"

"I don't think so. We shouldn't really be seen together. I am network and you are… you know."

"You know" came up often, as in *I can't go out with you Bender, I am an actress on your show. I am your real estate agent lawyer accountant trainer yoga instructor masseuse secretary jogging partner dentist sound editor; it would be inappropriate.* The occupations of eligible women in Hollywood were down to Los Angeles Zookeeper or Trader Joe's Team Member.

"Why don't we pick up sushi and go back to your house?" Dulcie said.

"Sounds great," Bender said.

For now, he agreed to keep the affair that wasn't yet an affair a secret. Friday night the sushi soured in its bento box while they had their first bout of impatient sex. Afterward he and Dulcie ate microwaved pizza in the hot tub. In the morning, they watched raccoons fight over bits of floating mozzarella.

Christine

The sign over the door only had enough light bulbs to spell *Wag Whe l*. A rusted iron grate covered foggy front windows. Inside things got better. A Frederick Remington reproduction *Fight for the Waterhole* hung over the long bar; wooden tables sat under wagon-wheel light chandeliers. Framed autographed photos of cowboy actors lined the walls: Gene Autry, Roy and Dale, Hopalong Cassidy, Randolph Scott, Joel McCrea, Tom Mix, John Wayne, then the next wave of gunslingers: Lee Van Cleef, Steve McQueen, Lorne Greene, Chuck Connors, and Clint Eastwood; it was a mosaic of Stetsons, embroidered shirts, Colts, lariats, and guitars.

In a back room there was a dance floor, an upright piano on a small bandstand where square dancing couples in pointed boots, and calico dresses did do-si-dos and allemande lefts.

Bender spotted two city bus drivers at the bar, a postal worker, three downtown artists, a little man in a pork pie hat; his arm halfway around the waist of a woman in a pink pant suit, who looked like she weighed at least three hundred pounds. The only female in the Wagon Wheel, she must be his date, Christine Deutsch. For a moment, and only a moment, he considered leaving but he heard Dale telling him, "Do the right thing, pardner."

"Christine?" he said.

The woman twisted around on her bar stool. A blonde beehive rose like an artillery shell to the ceiling. She swung a pink forearm into the chest of the little man in the porkpie hat. "I told you he'd show up. Now beat it."

She indicated the vacant barstool. "Pull up a seat, Mr. Bender. I'm Christine. What are you drinking?"

She was beautiful. Her face contained the essence of all of Bender's past loves, Judy Mancuso in the fifth grade, Kim Novak in high school, Botticelli's Venus in college, though one glance at her body told him a scallop shell would crumble beneath it. She smiled white, Bender knew it was worth the detour to the Wagon Wheel for here, on Alvarado Street, was surely the promise of an adventure.

Dulcie

Bender and Dulcie were now in a full-blown clandestine romance. They met in restaurants where no one knew them, or they ordered take-out dinners at his house. He took appropriate measures, embracing his new-found monogamy.

As for his gone wife Ellen, Bender knew his obsession was merely on hold, he was a co-conspirator in his own fiction that life had two possibilities: this new woman, Dulcie, was the cure for his heartache, or Ellen would come to her senses and return to Bender. If that happened, he'd find a way to extricate himself from Dulcie, as gently as possible. Bender was aware that he was still unfit for human consumption but as a compartmentalizer he put his pain aside while he found a new woman to distract him. The more neurotic the woman, the better the distraction.

"Bender, you haven't called me in a week. Are you in love?" Mimi said.

"I don't know."

"Who is she?"

"I can't say yet."

"Married?"

"No."

"Movie star?"

"No."

"So what's the secret?"

"She works for ABC, assigned to my show. We're just being discreet for a while. It's refreshing."

In his bedroom that night, Dulcie said, "Bender, do you think somebody is following you?"

He turned on the light. Dulcie was wearing a thin UCLA t-shirt.

"Someone is following me?"

"I was just thinking."

The next morning, as she was dressing, Bender said, "Why would someone be following me?"

"I don't know. Maybe we should ease off a little bit. Not see each other as much. Or at least not here."

"Why not here?"

"My ex. I think he knows where you live."

Christine

The little man in the pork pie hat moved down the bar, found another stool, keeping an eye on Bender and Christine in the mirror behind the rows of liquor. Bender tried to keep an eye on him in return, but his face was hidden by a large bottle of rum. Christine? He wanted to know everything about the answering service. Hours worked, pay, customers, good ones, jerks, doctors, any other show business clients? She bubbled on, they ate peanuts, jerky sticks, microwaved nachos, kept the bartender busy pouring shots of vodka for him and tequila for Christine. She told him stories about Ace's clients but gave no names. He liked that; it meant his own was safe. Ace's office was in Beverly Hills; there was the issue of parking.

"I use the lot behind Saks."

"Pretty expensive, isn't it?"

"Tell me about it. I gotta blow the guy who runs the place once a week to let me park for free."

"I see."

Bender was tipsy, the Wagon Wheel was quiet; the man in the pork pie hat was rolling dice for drinks with the mailman, the bus drivers were staring up at a lucha libre wrestling match on a soundless television set.

"Okay, Bender, it's my turn for questions."

Like a cinematographer with a Steadicam, he leaned back on his barstool away from Christine so he could take her in, she was too large for a close-up, even a medium shot, the frame couldn't contain her, he needed distance.

Bender cocked his head, offering an ear. "Okay. Ask away."

"Tell me what it's like to be a writer."

"Why?"

"Maybe I'll try it when I get to Phoenix. What's the secret?"

"A good pen."

"You're a wise guy, you know that?"

Shamed, he moved closer. "Okay. Reading writing, arithmetic, forget the arithmetic. Ernest Hemingway, Dorothy Parker and Mickey Spillaney. Read them, the rest is up to you." He grabbed a handful of peanuts, drank the last of his vodka.

"What else do you want to know?"

"Are you Jewish, Bender?"

"Yes."

"You ever had sex with anybody as big as me?"

Dulcie

She chose an Armenian restaurant in Glendale. "You haven't told anyone about us, have you?"

"Of course not."

"Josh Rosen?" The director of Bender's sitcom.

"No."

"Are you seeing Dulcie Keller?" Josh asked.

"Yes. But don't tell anyone."

"What about Bari, your assistant?" Dulcie asked.

"No way."

"Are you having a thing with Dulcie Keller?" Bari asked.

"Yes. But I'm keeping it quiet."

Bender had to tell Cousin Iris because he told her everything, also lawyer Dennis, but no one else, except delicatessen Steve.

"Does she have a name?" Steve asked.

"Why, does it matter?"

"Just curious."

"Dulcie Keller. Don't tell anyone."

There was the Saturday morning when his yoga teacher arrived early, surprising them on the deck wrapped in bath towels.

"She won't tell anyone."

"Why did you have to introduce me? Now she knows my name."

"Don't worry. She's a celebrity yoga instructor. She can't discuss her clients. She's like a psychiatrist."

And he had to tell Dr. Grotstein. "I think I met someone."

"Congratulations. Does she have a name?"

"Dulcie Keller."

"I'll add her to the list."

Christine

Jack Jackson entered the Wagon Wheel, saw Bender, and didn't see him. An actor, composer, playwright, he was also the artistic director of the Pico Union Cultural Center. He walked past Bender, concluding with Euclidian finality, "I see Bender at the bar whispering into the ear of a 300-pound woman in a pink pants suit with a Wilma Flintstone hairdo. *Quod erat demonstrandum*: it is not Bender."

Bender realized he had become Ralph Ellison's *Invisible Man*. Jack, a Black man, didn't see him. It might be interesting, but Bender wasn't sure how it played out in terms of current racial politics. Jack sat down at a table against the wall, emptied his briefcase of legal pads, a bunch of pens in a rubber band, opened a script, began writing. Bender remembered why he knew about the Wagon Wheel; it was Jack's 'office.' "I go there to work. I get an empty table, drink sherry, no one bothers me."

Bender turned to Christine. "Will you excuse me for a moment?"

"Sure. If it's the men's, make a right at Joel McCrea."

He walked unsteadily to Jack's table, planted his feet.

"Bender? What are you doing here?"

"A date."

"No shit, who's the lucky lady?"

"The blonde at the bar in the pink suit."

Jack swung around in his chair for a look. "That one?"

"Yup."

"Cool, good for you."

When Bender returned to his barstool, he caught the little man in the pork pie hat checking him, ready to make a move on Christine if Bender passed out. Christine leaned in and found his ear with her tongue, "Let's get out of here, Bender."

Outside the Wagon Wheel, standing next to Christine, Bender measured her, she was only an inch shorter than him; he was six-one.

"Where'd you park?" she said.

"I found a spot on Alvarado."

"Leave it there. I'm just around the corner."

Christine walked gracefully alongside him, humming "Yesterday," the song playing on the jukebox as they left the Wagon Wheel. He was stupid drunk, his mind a chewed olive pit. He had no idea how this would end, but it was the part of life he liked best. The not knowing. For him, climbing a mountain was exciting because there was something unknown on the other side. A dress was a curtain to be pulled back, a bra to be snapped open, somewhere in this pink and yellow mass of a woman was a door, if he could find it. A moment later, it might have been a crack in the sidewalk, an earthquake, or too much vodka, he tripped, lurched forward. Christine grabbed his wrist, keeping him from splitting his head on the concrete or floating to the sky over the spires of the Union Church of Los Angeles.

"Thanks."

"Sure."

Here on this deserted street in Pico Union, in downtown Los Angeles, the home of the Western Locos, the Dog Town Rifa, the Crazy Riders, gangs who shot first and didn't bother to ask questions, a warm feeling came over him. Bender glanced sideways at Christine's body next to his; the barrel-like shape of her torso, rounds of flesh flowing out of her armpits into her breasts, all of it mounted on massive thighs, her determined alert face, pug nose perfectly placed on apple cheeks. He heard Dr. Grotstein: "Tell me, Bender, what did you feel at that moment?"

"I felt safe." Before he began to cry, Bender said, "I think for me, safe is love."

Dulcie

There were clues, inklings, intimations. Why had he never been in Dulcie's apartment? Why did her car, a battered Mazda convertible, look like it had rolled over a couple of times? Why, as a birthday present, did she give him a setting of silverware she had stolen from the Polo Lounge? Why did she ask him if he was being followed? Why did she ask him before sex if he liked mild torture, either inflicted by her or by him? Bender chose to ignore all these signs. Why? Was it because he tended to perceive insanity as interesting? Was it because interesting was attractive?

After the dress rehearsal Bender made small talk with the cast, then climbed up to the bleachers where Dulcie was waiting for him, script on her lap, ready to give notes.

"It's fine. I mean, more than fine. I don't really have anything to say."

"Good. That's an early day for me, then. Dinner, tonight? I liked that hotel on the beach. We could walk to the Venice pier."

She bit her lip, tilted her head, and, like an undirected actress indicating sadness, delivered her line:

"I can't see you anymore."

"What?"

She added a shake of the head, closed her eyes for a moment, recited the reasons, none of which he could remember clearly. There was no point. Of all the lessons his mother preached, from 'wear clean underwear in the event of an automobile accident' to 'smile when you are on the phone,' the only one he took to heart was 'no is no.' This was a useful survival strategy for a writer in Hollywood where rejections were as common as ants at a picnic. When Navitz told him a producer had turned down a screenplay he never asked why. No is no. There was one exception: no is no did not apply to Ellen. It would take more than his mother's admonition for him to give up the why. In Dulcie's libretto of breaking up, the reasons were many. Later, he tried to recall them:

Did Dulcie say:

"I was in a relationship that had ended but it turns out that we started talking about getting back together because it turns out that we still love each other so it's not fair to you while I am really not out of it, emotionally."

Or:

"It's not going to work. You are creative, I'm network, this is jeopardizing my career. It's just not done. You really ought to think about dating a pharmacist."

Or:

"We don't want the same things. You want children, a family. I don't."

Or:

The truth, she did not say. "I'm hooked on theatre, Bender, though not the kind you see at The Mark Taper. My boyfriend is a writer, too, but his plots are scary. They require a leading man. You. We love each other but he is extremely controlling, he likes to use his fists. When I can't take it anymore, I leave him, find a nice new boyfriend. This time, it was you. But I miss him, and I go back. Of course, he punishes me for being a bad girl, so together we punish the boyfriend. You. If you know what's good for you, run. But you won't. Stay tuned."

Christine

Her apartment looked like a dressing room in an Amazonian strip club. Cannon ball bras, panties the size of kitchen towels, sweat socks hung from cupboard knobs, dresses that could pass for body bags draped over furniture, mismatched shoes and sneakers piled in a corner.

"The couch opens up to a bed."

"Very clever."

"Make yourself at home." She turned on the radio. "You like jazz? Rock? Country?"

Bender pushed a garment bag aside, sat on a corner of the couch. "Jazz."

Christine found Chuck Niles on KKJZ, sat down next to him, taking up the rest of the couch. "Should we do it? Or get high first?"

He was ambivalent about sex with Christine. For the first time in his adult life, he did not know where to begin. "Let's get high."

Christine raised one thigh off the couch, searched under the cushion. "You used to get your weed from Jimmy Watson, right?"

"You knew him?"

"Not personally but we had a lot of clients who bought from him."

She produced a plastic bag of marijuana and papers. "You roll. I hated the system he used. All that shit with codes, satellite numbers. You'd think we were dealing with nuclear secrets. What happened to him?"

"He died."

"Oh, that's fucked. Is Annette okay?"

"You knew her, too?"

"She had her own account. But that's as far as I'm going."

They smoked the joint that Bender rolled and listened to Sonny Rollins.

Christine grew up in a mobile home park outside of Hemet.

"We were not trailer trash. It was a doublewide lot, more than just fine. My sister and I had our own bedrooms. There was a swimming pool, a senior center, and the nicest neighbors you could want. My descent to trash came later. I was married four times; would you believe it?"

Four men who loved her. "Tell me about them."

"Bobby was a musician, Mr. Jazz Piano, I called him. He is not the one who got me into drugs, that was number four. Mr. Jazz Piano came home after gigs, sang me his solos, played them on my belly with his fingers, oh, oh, by the time he finished I was wet. One day he stopped playing me, so I knew he was playing somebody else, which turned out to be true. Number two, Mr. Lawyer was a fast mistake, but he lied on the marriage license, so it was easy to get it annulled.

I was also pregnant which I didn't know until after we got annulled. Go chase a lawyer for money, hah. Number three, Mr. Antonio, was a sweetheart. Had a little upholstery business but he got killed in a robbery. Wasn't even him they were robbing; it was a fabric cutter down the hall. Antonio heard some noise, went to see what it was and bang, they shot him, too. From then on, I hear a noise, I stay where I am. Are you hungry? I could call Domino's."

"I'm good. Number four?"

"Earl. We're still married. He's the one who got me into drugs, but I take responsibility, too. We went through U-Turn For Christ, got sober, except for weed, in my case. He was working with them in LaVerne when our son Pablo got cancer. In the meantime, Mr. Lawyer woke up one day, said he wanted to have a relationship with his son. But like a lot of things in life, it came too late."

"I'm sorry."

"Yeah. Me, too."

Dulcie

Getting dumped by Dulcie was painful. Bender knew what would follow: depression, loneliness, sexual jealousy; he would miss her, picture her in someone's embrace, enjoying life while he didn't. But in some corner of his mind, he also knew it would pass, he'd get over her and go back to missing Ellen. He might even come to view this one as a case of Cupid balancing the books. Dr. Grotstein counted that as progress.

Bender spent the next week working on his sitcom. On run-through day, Dulcie sent her assistant to cover the show; at the notes session she was diplomatic, obviously she had been told not to have too many opinions.

Bari said, "I have Dulcie Keller for you on one."

He closed the door of his office.

"Nora told me the run-through was great," she said.

"Thanks. Listen, about the other day. Maybe we should talk."

"I'd rather not. I just wanted to know if you've heard from anyone."

"Who are you talking about?"

"Any weird phone calls?"

"No."

"Okay, I have to go. Good luck on the taping."

"Will you be there?" he said to a dial tone.

o   o   o

That evening Bender got a phone call. A man.

"You know what you did to her, don't you?"

"Who is this?"

"You really messed her up. Now you're going to have to pay."

"Pay?"

"You can't hurt people, destroy their lives, and expect not to be punished. I know everything about you; you will be easy. Get ready to die."

Hang up.

In the early morning of his solid sleep, he dreamed of a ship: a black freighter in the calm waters of Santa Monica bay, its guns trained on The Ivy restaurant on Ocean Boulevard where Bender stood, ignored, at the hostess's altar as people swept past him. He peered past them into the dining room where they circled around a naked body lying on a buffet table. Bender saw a producer who had fired him, an actor who changed all his lines, a studio accountant who fixed it so his show earned no profits. A shadowy male figure stood behind them, his face out of focus, a Marine Corps bayonet in his hand. Bender looked at the naked body, it was him, lying on his back, skin taut and chalk white. There was a white towel around his waist, Neil Navitz was probing his genitals under the towel with a stick. He knew, even as this nightmare unfolded, that the setting of this dream was not his own. Dr. Grotstein suggested he dreamed in stolen scenarios.

"You are Little Hans with a heavy dose of plagiarism."

What had he borrowed this time? Of course, Rembrandt's *Anatomy Lesson*. Neil Navitz was Dr. Nicolaes Tulp, explaining the musculature of limp dicks to a showbiz crowd. The man with the bayonet stood up and pushed Navitz aside. A Chuck Close box of squares obscured his face. He raised the bayonet. Another Bender, the one without a reservation, tried to break through the crowd but the hostess blocked his path. "We don't have a table for you. You are hereby banned from the Ivy."

Bender was escorted outside to Ocean Avenue by security guards. He looked out to the Pacific. A motor launch full of armed men was lowered from the black freighter, then put-putted its way to the Santa Monica Pier. The men disembarked and silently marched to the Ivy. An officer in a black beret, carrying a machine pistol saluted him.

"Your orders, Mr. Bender?"

"Bring out the patrons. All of them."

"Kill them now or later?" The captain asked.

With mercy shown to some and not to others, especially the man with the Marine bayonet, Bender said, "Right now! Also, the hostess."

The phone was ringing him out of his dream, but he squeezed an extra second in and yelled, "That'll learn ya!"

Bender awoke to the overture of *The Threepenny Opera*, his dream another plagiarism.

The voice on the phone said, "I know where you live. I know the inside of your house; I know how to kill you. Have a nice day, Bender."

Hang up.

Christine

Bender's dreams were hard to define, they were abstract head-jerking fragments of suns, microbes, Baja roads, crushed paper, images rushing past him like fast cuts in a film. When he awoke, Christine was asleep on the floor. Bender tried to move her to the couch, it was impossible. He put a pillow under her head. She had been telling him about Pablo, her son who lived in Phoenix. "It was the sun. He could never get enough. It was just a spot at first and when you are young you don't go to the doctor, he didn't have anybody to tell him to, so by the time he did, it was too late. Twenty-eight, it breaks my heart. Earl, that's my ex, was working in Vegas but quit to take care of Pablo. He sent me a ticket and said best for us all to be together as the sky turns black. Do you believe in God? I don't remember you getting phone calls from rabbis."

"No."

"What's the matter Bender, you look like you got problems."

"I do."

"Well, let's hear them, big boy. Take my mind off mine."

Bender told her about crazy Dulcie, the death threats. She nodded, still stoned, trying to stay awake. "I'm listening, really," but her eyes closed, she slowly rolled off the couch back onto the floor. Should he wake her, as she snored little snorts in her smiling sleep? Was she dreaming of pushing five-year-old Pablo on a swing, higher Mommy higher Mommy, or was she dreaming of Hemet and her trailer park home? Bender decided not to wake her. It was three in the morning; he was clear headed. Time to go. He was patting his pockets for keys when he heard the noise; three discrete cracks, unmistakably gunshots. He bent down next to Christine, shook her shoulder.

One eye opened. "What is it, honey?"

"I heard gunshots outside."

"What time is it?"

"Three."

"Yeah. Welcome to the neighborhood."

Bender calculated his car was a ten-minute walk from her apartment. "Can I sleep on the couch?"

"Sure."

"You said you had advice for me."

"About the crazy guy who wants to kill you?"

"Yes."

Her eye closed. Was she trying to remember or was she going back to sleep? She shook her head, her eye opened. "Buy a gun, shoot the motherfucker."

"I have a gun, but I don't think I can bring myself to use it."

"Christine said. "I'll find somebody to do it for you."

Dulcie

Dulcie told Bender the phone caller wasn't her ex-boyfriend after all, but a crazy writer who had also been stalking her. She didn't know his name; said she had asked to be assigned to another show so they wouldn't be seeing each other anymore. She wished him luck and hung up.

That evening, the phone call; same voice, "Bender?"

"Yeah?"

"You told people you were sleeping with Dulcie. You hurt her. I need to get even. Even you can understand that."

Hang up.

Phone rings.

Don't answer.

Practice finding shotgun under bed.

Check door locks, check windows.

Phone rings. Phone rings. Phone rings.

Don't answer.

Watch TV.

Fall asleep.

Phone rings.

Answer.

"You hung up on me, fucker. I'm coming over to end your miserable life."

Hang up.

A week later the salesman at Retting's Gun Depot called Bender and told him his handgun application was approved; the Smith & Wesson Magnum was waiting. Bender wrote a check for $1500, bringing his total arms expenditure to $3,500, not including ammunition. At home, despite his arsenal, Bender felt less safe. What if the mystery caller also had a gun? What if his gun was better? More expensive? Bender began carrying the Smith & Wesson to the bathroom. In the shower he placed the gun on the soap dish in case he was attacked like Janet Leigh in *Psycho*. Then there was the fear that he would wake up in the middle of the night in a massive depression and shoot himself.

That night there was a frantic banging on his front door. Bender grabbed the Benelli.

Two more bangs on the door.

He looked out through the peephole. The taillight of a car disappeared. A few minutes later his phone rang. Bender cradled the Benelli and let it ring.

o   o   o

Bari said, "I have a man on the line who wants to talk to you, but he won't give me his name."

"Hang up."

"He wants to leave a message."

"Hang up."

A moment later Bari entered his office. "He said he's going to kill you."

"It's a wrong number," Bender said.

Dennis Roberts

"Forget guns," lawyer Dennis said. "What you want is information and humiliation. You want revenge, civil litigation is the only way to go."

"Are you going to do it?"

"I'd love to, but it's better if you use someone in L.A. I'll find somebody for you. You want a merciless, grab 'em by the balls lawyer."

Fiona Ballard

She spoke so softly Bender had to lean forward to hear her. Was Fiona, hair in a bun, wire-rimmed glasses, who bore an uncanny resemblance to Emily Dickinson, the right lawyer to instill fear and trembling into a pair of Hollywood socio-paths?

"I will make her life a fucking living hell," Fiona chirped. "The question is how much hell can you afford?"

"I'm only interested in finding out who the caller is," Bender said.

"We need to squeeze her. The distance between the vagina and the anus is millimeters but it can seem like a mile."

"I beg your pardon?"

"She knows his name," Fiona said. "She won't tell you. Why? Either she loves him or she's afraid of him; if it's the latter I can help her, if she loves him, I'll carve her a new one."

Bender wrote a retainer check for slightly less than the cost of the Benelli.

Dear Ms. Keller,

I represent David Bender. A person known to you has caused Mr. Bender extreme mental duress though repeated threats on his life. I am assisting the L.A. Police Department in their investigation of this crime. If it should turn out that any of his phone calls were made in your presence, or from your telephone, you would be aiding and abetting this crim-inal conduct. You will also be named a co-defendant in the civil litigation to be brought against your demonic associate. You can, within twenty-four hours of receipt of this letter, reveal this person's name and address to Mr. Bender, or me, or you can face the situation outlined above.

Fiona Ballard, Attorney at Law

A few days later Bender received another letter.

Dear Mr. Bender,

Dulcie is my sister. Adam Spicer is the person who is calling you. He's a television producer like you. He was dating Dulcie. In August they broke up, then she met you. Alan threatened her so she dropped you and went back to him. Please go easy on Dulcie, she is a victim of this sick individual, she doesn't have the strength to go up against him. She hopes you will call off your lawyer. I hope you do, too.

Sincerely,

Barbara Keller, Dulcie's sister.

His potential assassin was a card-carrying member of the Writers Guild. That night, Bender answered the phone, smiled as his mother taught him. "Hello," he said.

"Bender, I'm going to kill you tomorrow. Are you ready to die?"

"Hey, Adam. Adam Spicer, right? Tomorrow's not good. Back-to-back network meetings. How about Wednesday? I could pencil you in."

Christine, Dulcie, Bender

They sat at Jack Jackson's table in the Wagon Wheel. Bender, Christine, and Dulcie. What did the little man in the porkpie hat see from his perch at the bar? He saw his beautiful Christine sitting next to the Beverly Hills asshole who stole her from him. There was another woman, a skinny blonde, nervous, biting her lip. Christine was doing the talking. If he was seated at the table, the little man in the porkpie hat would hear:

"Listen, Dulcie," Christine said, "I know the whole story. I think Bender's version of what went down is very generous. He sees you as a victim, but personally I see you and your sick fuck boyfriend as partners in this little game. But now that we know his name, Adam Spicer, I have a message for you to give him. Bender has taken out a contract on his life. I arranged it. Money already paid. In this economy it isn't that expensive. So, if anything ever happens to him, including automobile accidents, then your little piece of shit boyfriend Spicer is dead. Understand? Why Bender didn't include you in the deal is an act of kindness, but that's his business. You got it?"

The little man in the porkpie hat saw the skinny blonde nod her head. He saw Christine and the Beverly Hills asshole walk to the door. They were holding hands. The little man in the porkpie hat knew the expression, but he was still surprised to find himself crying in his beer.

On the sidewalk, Bender said to Christine, "Thank you."

"Stay in touch. If he calls again, let me know."

"He won't."

"You really giving me the down payment for the condo?"

"I sold my guns. I can afford it."

"You don't need guns. You have a good heart, that's enough."

Christine drew Bender into her softness and kissed him. She tasted of Wagon Wheel peanuts.

"My life is pretty crazy, don't you agree?" Bender said.

"It's a life, Bender. We only get one. Be kind to it."

They went off in opposite directions to their cars. This is what people do in Los Angeles, Bender thought. They drive away. He ran to Christine.

"Hey, Bender, what's up?'

"Nothing much. I'll walk you to your car."

SANTA MONICA
BOULEVARD

Bender stared at the caricatures on the walls of The Palm restaurant, wondering if the size of one's portrait could be considered a measure of success in Hollywood. Bender reconsidered; the thought was banal at best and at worst inaccurate. The fading drawings were of an earlier time and no Navitz Artists agent or Sam Cohn client would allow their face to be placed between an obscure USC quarterback and a long dead business manager to the stars. But there was a cartoon image of Bender's producer Sidney Beckerman, sporting a fifties pompadour, an exaggerated square jaw clenching a cigar, posed behind a camera operator, ready to jump in and adjust the frame. Sidney was also known for holding the record of the number of dishes named for him on menus in Hollywood restaurants; *Steak Diablo Sidney* at Matteo's, *Beckerman's Sky High* at Art's Deli (tongue, turkey and pastrami with a schmear of chopped liver) and, until he sucker punched Bobby Littman at Ma Maison, *Blanquette de Veau James with Blanquette de Veau Sidney Beckerman* was a Wolfgang Puck specialty. It was removed as part of the settlement. Bender's lunch with Sidney was meant to discuss directors for Bender's screenplay adaptation of a novel owned by Universal. It was assigned to Bender in a baroque chain of favors returned, debts paid, and silences rewarded.

It began when Barbara Ganz, the wife of a Vice President at Universal, had an idea for a sitcom and invited her best friend Tanya Ellis who was married to the head of the literary department at Navitz Artists to write it with her. They did, and with both husbands too cowardly to say 'no,' it made its way to CBS where the development team, knowing from whence it came, quickly hired a writer (Bender) to do a polish (a complete rewrite). The premise of the pilot – a divorcee with two teenage daughters who moves back into her mother's house – was acceptable, but the script itself was amateurish, as two amateurs wrote it.

Bender's agent, Neil, seeing a way to get Barbara's husband in his debt, convinced Bender to do an uncredited, unpaid, rewrite as a favor that would be rewarded, *trust me*. Bender's version worked, a pilot was produced and picked up for the CBS fall schedule. Like bank robbers after a successful heist, the loot was divided. Barbara and Tanya got a show on the air, Bender was handed the lucrative assignment to adapt a novel at Universal, and Sidney, for agreeing to hire Bender, would be the producer. Sidney balked at first, Bender was a *television* writer as opposed to a *film* writer, but the promise of a go movie and a hefty producer's fee changed his mind. The Vice President of Universal, hoping to populate the film with cast members from *Saturday Night Live* hired a director who made short films for the show, unaware that Bill Murray, Dan Ackroyd, and John Belushi hated him and subsequently refused to appear in the film.

Sidney fired the director. For his replacement, the wheels turned. The director of Barbara and Tanya's pilot was reluctant to direct the series episodes. He was a pilot director, so when the job of directing Sidney's movie was offered to him, and seeing a path from TV to film, he relented and did the first thirteen episodes of the series.

Sidney slid into the booth, plucked a toothpick from a shot glass and began to search for remaining bits of steak hiding in his gleaming white teeth. "Bender, I have bad news about our director."

"The steak was delicious, Sidney. I can handle bad news."

"I talked to him yesterday. He never had sex in his office."

"You can't be serious."

"And it gets worse. He's never had sex with more than one person at a time. We are in big trouble. He is a man with a thirty-minute sitcom mind and no balls." Bender swallowed his own lies; he had never had sex in his office or a threesome. On the other hand, Sidney was legendary; he was rumored to have the largest penis in Hollywood and was once challenged in the men's room of Chasen's by Milton Berle. Sidney won, and said later, "I only showed him enough to win."

Sidney skewered a cold onion ring, considered, then tossed it back on the plate. "It's my fault, Bender. I never should have allowed the studio to put him on my picture. I don't understand the way it works at Universal. Whose cock am I supposed to suck? Do you know?"

"Well, at least he likes the script," Bender said.

"So what? He'll fuck it up. We have to get rid of him. Trust me, I'll find a way to get him off the picture. We still have a few weeks before we start pre-production."

Off the picture? Bender thrilled to the prospect of getting a director fired. Years of forced rewrites, and autocratic changes by self-styled *geniuses* with DGA cards had turned Bender from an idealistic collaborator to the equivalent of a film bigot.

On the other hand, Sidney was the last person Bender would trust even though he knew Sidney wasn't talking about *personal* trust. He meant *show business* trust, which was different. He remembered his first meeting with Sidney. "*Trust* me," he said. "If I can find a way not to screw you on this deal I won't, but if I can't then God bless." It was only a week later when Bender was again lunching at The Palm, this time invited by a producer who needed a re-write of a screenplay. During the lunch Sidney ambled over to their table. He stood behind Bender and massaged his shoulders. Sidney said, "You like this guy?"

"Yes."

"He's a good writer, this Bender."

"Yes, he is," the producer said.

"Good. Because you can have him."

"I beg your pardon?"

Still massaging Bender's shoulders Sidney said, "He's yours. He's off the picture. You hear that, Bender, you fucking traitor? You cocksucker. You're fired. You're off the picture."

He released Bender's shoulders, gave them a farewell pat and returned to his table.

I'm off the picture, Bender thought. Where had he heard that before? He remembered it was how Sidney fired people. Now what? Navitz would also be at lunch. He turned to his host.

"I feel like he caught me in bed with his wife."

"You're waiting for a green light from the studio on your picture at Universal, right?"

"Right."

"So, nothing's happening. Sidney doesn't own you. You're allowed to take meetings. Don't worry about it."

Bender returned to his office. Bari said, "I have Sidney Beckerman for you."

"Hello, Sidney."

"Bender, I spend my mornings yelling and my afternoons apologizing. Okay?"

Bender realized he wasn't getting an apology, so he just said, "Okay."

"We're good?" Sidney said.

"Yes."

"Okay. I think I found a way to get rid of our director."

THE CARIBBEAN

Bender, hiding in his stateroom on the *Sea Bream*, was desperate. There was nothing to read, he was too depressed to write. He had watched all the movies on the ship's entertainment channel, the rest consisted of a video tour of the ship, *Wild Kingdom* reruns, an Israeli channel streaming Knesset debates, and a continuous loop of sermons by Rabbi Schneerson in Yiddish. Fucked he was. *Dope, jerk, putz, idiot, pea brain, dunce, yutz.* Bender ran out of words to describe himself. Why didn't he mention Isaac Singer who when he was asked whether Yiddish was a dead language said, "It is true that there is no word for jet plane in Yiddish but there are forty words for fool." Why couldn't Bender relate that anecdote to his audience instead of a sarcastic, incendiary idea for a screenplay?

Whose fault was this? He picked at an onion matzoh in his breakfast basket, searched the recesses of his petty, vindictive mind for a scapegoat. Is Louise, his latest distraction from Ellen, was a candidate. Had he boarded a Passover cruise to avoid her Seder? Possibly. Bender's recent decision to boycott Jewish holiday celebrations was starting to take its toll on their relationship; it was also poisoning their sex life. She was vaguely agnostic (*there must be something out there*) but holiday observant. Bender's refusal to participate in Jewish rituals was beginning to turn her off.

"For me sex is a way of expressing trust."

"You don't trust me because I won't eat bitter herbs and hide matzos?"

"It's not about that. The Seder is only a symbol of a deeper problem."

"Such as?"

"Inability to commit. To do the work."

The work. How many times had Bender heard that word? Marriage is work, love is work, actors' agents say it's all about the work. The actors Bender knew talked about the money. Louise believed in the continuity, the efficacy of psychotherapy. She prodded him relentlessly to resolve his conflicts with Judaism that were related to trust issues; 'you have to do the work on the couch.' He was no stranger to green leather, but he was on hiatus from his twice-weekly visits to Dr. Grotstein. Louise's own therapist saw his avoidance of Jewish holidays and dietary strictures as a mask of deeper unresolved issues related to his mother. In short: get shrunk, get Jewish, get laid. The better solution was to lie. Bender told Louise he was returning to work with Dr. Grotstein; he was careful not to answer his phone on Thursday mornings from ten to eleven in the event she called. Occasionally, he would provide her with illuminating painful memories extracted by Dr. Grotstein that pointed the way to a reunion with his Jewish heritage based on an insight that his mother was a controlling Sarah figure.

In his cabin, staring at the unchanging sea, he had also considered the idea of a free vacation, an all-expense-paid cruise that began with a call from Stu Weintraub, a former agent who was now booking entertainment for specialty cruises, ones that offered yoga, investment advice, weight loss, dialysis, quilting, substance abuse, and his latest, The Glatt Kosher Passover Cruise aboard the *Sea Bream.* It featured two full Seders at sea, led by the legendary Rabbi Howard Zuker. There were Jewish scholars and authors for lectures; a stunning array of guest cantors: Hyman Berger, Daniel Tartikov, the legendary blind Cantor of Lodz, Yehuda Salitzkovitz. The executive chef of the Jerusalem Hilton, Seth Rokah prepared Passover dishes, his kosher kitchen supervised by Rabbi Avi Rosenshein. *The Sea Bream* sailed the warm blue waters of the Caribbean with stops in Martinique, Labadee, Montego Bay, and San Juan.

Stu needed someone for two nights of family entertainment.

"I got the intellectuals, the wonks, but I need someone for the parents and kids," he said.

Bender had written the screenplay for *What Would Sandy Do?*, a movie about a Little League team that was sponsored by a synagogue. The team makes it to the state championship only to be faced with a religious dilemma; the final game is scheduled for Saturday. Inspired by the story of the great Dodger pitcher Sandy Koufax, who refused to play in a World Series game on Yom Kippur, the team votes to forfeit the Saturday game. Just as they are about to convey their decision to the league there is a sudden rainstorm, the game is moved to Sunday. The kids see this as a miracle, a message from God. He wants them to play; He made it rain. They play Sunday and lose. The kids are devastated, certain that God has abandoned them. Coach Rabbi Aaron tells them God gave them the opportunity to play but winning was something they had to do themselves. Heartwarming, funny, the film became a classic in Jewish cinema, a staple in suburban synagogues.

"You screen *What Would Sandy Do?*, followed by a Q and A going out, on the return you show them your remake of *A Dog of Flanders*. It's set in the Louisiana Bayou, right? You get nine days on the *Sea Bream* in a first-class cabin."

Louise couldn't join Bender; she was committed to her sister's Seder but considered the Passover cruise as spiritual progress. "It's not whose Seder, but a Seder," she said.

Neil Navitz pronounced Bender's spec screenplay saleable. "I'll send it to our directors, but you should be aware that everyone in town is getting ready for Passover, then it's Cannes. No one is reading. There is a tiny window between Cannes and Shavuot. That's the hole I'm aiming for, so this cruise might be a good way to get out of town, relax, take a break from writing. You can also think about your next project."

"Do I have to go to the Seders?" he asked Stu.

"Of course not. By the way, you do well on this cruise I can get you lots more. You'll never pay for a vacation again."

Bender pictured himself with Ellen, windswept on the bow of the *Sea Bream*; moonlight bouncing off the gentle waves of the Caribbean, once again in love.

"I'll take it."

Bender flew to Miami; a limo took him to a giant cruise ship that looked like an apartment building lying on its side. An officer in dress whites escorted him to the first-class lounge where a cocktail party was in progress. The captain introduced him to his fellow celebrities, who would provide intellectual nourishment on the cruise: Rabbi Stan Kirsch, whose lecture on the futility of the any-state solution was getting traction in AIPAC, Allen Didowitz on Anti-Semitism in the California University System, and Rich Mowbray of the *Jewish Journal* to discuss his recent book, *Why Be Jewish?* All three told Bender *What Would Sandy Do?* was one of their favorite movies.

o o o

When lights came up after the film, the captain gave Bender a glowing introduction, handed him a microphone and a stack of file cards.

Questions:

"Have your Jewish roots influenced your work?"

"How much anti-Semitism do you encounter in Hollywood on a day-to-day basis?"

"What inspired you to write 'What Would Sandy Do?'?"

"Who is your favorite Jewish writer?"

"Why doesn't Hollywood make more films about Jews?"

"Are most of your friends observant?"

Bender flipped through the cards, at the same time scanning the room for a woman, one with a husband at the casino, a candidate for a drink at the bar afterward. A sympathetic literary soul. The tall woman sitting between two teenage daughters, was her perfectly coiffed hair a wig? Was she orthodox? He checked her skirt length and saw knees; she would be observant at most; Rich Mowbray's wife? Or the doleful brunette on the aisle in a black sweater, a celebrity cantor's wife? He constructed her story: dragged along on the cruise by her husband, bored to shit, tired of the adulation of his fans, their indifference to her. Did she dream of *Quenelles Nantua* at Chez Georges while she was eating *Gefilte Fish Masada* on the *Sea Bream?*

"Mr. Bender?" The captain said.

"Sorry, I was lost in the questions. They're all terrific. I'll start with this one. Yes, being Jewish informs almost everything I do." A lie, aside from *What Would Sandy Do?* his Jewish themed credits were thin.

"Next, anti-Semitism? I have to say I have never personally encountered any acts of anti-Semitism in my career. We all get along as far as religion is concerned. The real conflict is between creative and business. Writers versus business affairs, but it has nothing to do with religion, we're all Jewish."

Bender read the next card. "Of course, the inspiration for *What Would Sandy Do?* was Koufax. He was a hero to every Jewish boy who loved baseball. And, I hope, girl." He looked up, the woman in the black sweater gave him a warm smile. "My favorite Jewish writer? Beside me?" Laughter. "Really, I don't consider myself a Jewish writer. I'm just a writer. But of those who are, I would have to say Grace Paley. Then Salinger, and lastly Moses because he was not only good, but he was also lucky. I wish God had handed me an instant bestseller."

Bender looked at the next question, *'Are most of your friends observant?'*

Most of his friends hadn't seen the inside of a synagogue since their bar mitzvahs. This could get tricky, better to ignore them, instead, spill some Hollywood gossip, an anecdote about Mel Brooks, mention Campbell Hall, an Episcopalian private school that closed on Yum Kippur. He needed to fill another fifteen minutes. "Hey, how about some questions from non-card writers?"

The woman on the aisle said, "What are you working on now?"

Ten minutes later two men in Security jackets escorted Bender to his stateroom. Bender wished he was on Dr. Grotstein's couch in Westwood, investigating the self-destructive knob in him that made him leap into the fire of failure instead of the swimming pool of success. Could he use that line in a script? No, it was crap. Dr. Grotstein would say, "How did you get there, Mr. Bender?"

It was the question, "What are you working on now?" and Bender's answer: "A father and son story. A camping trip that in one sense is a failure but brings them closer. An homage to Hemingway."

"That sounds interesting. Will it be a movie?"

"Perhaps."

A man in the first row, arms folded over a bulging stomach said, "Why don't you write something like *Anne Frank*, or *Exodus?*"

"Those are terrific films, but it's not really what I do."

"Why not?" The man swung his head left to right, then nodded to the audience. He'd show this Hollywood hack; make him squirm. "You can't write another movie about the same subject?"

"Of course, I can. It's just not a subject I want to tackle now."

"Maybe you didn't like *Exodus.*"

"I said I liked it. It was a great movie."

"Maybe you're all written out."

Written out? Who was this putz, where did he learn the expression universally used by studio executives when they fired writers? Maybe he had a nephew in the business. Bender sensed he was on the edge of the cliff. Now it was only a matter of stepping off. "Okay," he said, "You want to hear my idea for a movie about the Holocaust?"

The man nodded, held out his palms with a 'show me' smile.

"A small town in Idaho is broke. The city council decides to build a Holocaust museum so they can attract tourists."

There was a silence. Bender looked at the woman on the aisle. Was she amused?

"You think that's funny?" The voice of the man had turned gravelly.

"I didn't say it was a comedy."

"Then what is it?"

"It could be satire."

"Of what?"

"About how bigoted people will choose money over their beliefs."

The woman on the aisle raised her hand. Her voice was sympathetic. "Why don't you tell us what happens in the movie."

"Thank you. Well, what with twenty-odd museums competing for Holocaust material, there isn't much left, so they have to get inventive."

"Inventive?"

"They can't get oral histories because there are no Holocaust survivors in the town. They ask people to make up oral histories of what people might have told them. Then the mayor gets the idea to display Hitler's car. They find an old Mercedes, borrow a life-size cutout of Hitler from the local Aryan Brotherhood, hire a photographer to take a picture of you sitting next to Hitler in the back seat. There are pony rides for the kids, but they make all the pony handlers wear arm bands with swastikas sewn on by the Hell's Angels Lady's Auxiliary."

"That's satire?" The man said.

"I don't know," Bender said. "Are the armbands too much? I could take them out."

A few people were walking out, throwing angry stares in his direction. There was one hand raised; it was his chance to regain the good will of his audience.

"Yes?" Bender said.

The man stood up. He had thick gray hair with a part on his left side, wore tan Dockers, a no-iron white shirt with the collars outside his suit jacket in the style of early Israeli politicians. Bender recognized him from the captain's welcome party: Lawrence Meyers, neo-con radio host, columnist, lecturer, a man who never met a liberal who didn't remind him of Stalin.

"I must say, sir, that you are suggesting something that explains precisely what is wrong with, and morally absent in, Hollywood."

Bender was about to apologize, say it was just an idea, probably a bad one. Explain that writers have lots of ideas, they often reject them; tell him you are really working on a film that will show Meir Kahane in a positive light, suggest Harrison Ford to play him. But before he could, Meyers continued, "While I must say, sir, I enjoyed your movie *What Would Sandy Do?*, I ask myself if it is the same writer standing here, who mocks our values, our rituals, and yes, our history. It is what left-wing Hollywood does so well. Sadly, it makes a lot of money."

His voice was mellow, unctuous, NPR perfect, not a pause; his words flowed effortlessly like molten shit.

Meyers turned away from Bender, faced the dwindling audience. "Where Hollywood sees humor, others see tragedy, where Hollywood celebrates the so-called oppressed, we mourn the victims of their terrorism. Where Hollywood celebrates cynicism, nihilism, blatantly insults our spiritual values, we believe morality must be rooted in a belief in God."

Meyers shook his head sadly. Bender knew where he was now. In the Tijuana bullring. He was Toro Bender; wounded, neck muscles weakened by the stabs of the *banderilleros*. Now facing Matador Meyers, his end was near, he was pawing the dirt with shaky legs.

"I will be frank with you, sir, based on my long experience in studying the left-wing Hollywood entertainment community," Matador Meyers said, as he raised his *estoque* for the kill, "You are, sir, a self-hating Jew."

Silence. Then applause. Would Toro Bender sink to his knees, flip over on the carpet of the King David Theater in the *Sea Bream* or stand firm, fight to the end hoping Matador Meyers will ask the crowd to spare Toro Bender for his bravery and let him retire to the *estansza* and spend the rest of his life impregnating cows. Bender knew he had created a train wreck metaphor; better to drop Tijuana, stick to reality. It was a short-lived decision. He created another: this one inspired by some genomic Eastern European memory of his grandfather, a tailor in the garment district of New York. Bender was two bolts of cloth. One was soft, silky, diplomatic, forgiving, non-confrontational. The other was rough, a thick weaved gabardine. He would be that one. He faced Meyers. "No, I am not a self-hating Jew. I love myself; I love Jews. Everyone in my family is one, except for the adopted daughter of my Aunt Tilly and Uncle Adolph. You know what? She became a rabbi. I'll tell you something else; I am the guy who turned down an all-expense paid trip to the Cairo Film Festival because I refused to put on the visa application that I was a Buddhist. Go fuck yourself."

o   o   o

In his stateroom Bender wondered how soon he could get off the *Sea Bream*, and whether he could turn the idea of an Idaho town with a Holocaust Museum into a screenplay. Pitch it to Bernie Brillstein for John Belushi as the town's mayor? He sketched a plot: in the beginning, the local white supremacists object to the museum, but when they see tourists come in droves from Coeur d'Alene and notice how the town's economy is revived, they change their minds. Thanks to the Holocaust museum, the town evolves into a more tolerant community. The climax is a festive meal in a pine *sukkah* built by burly members of the Aryan Nation with Belushi leading the service in Hebrew.

There was a soft knock at the door. Bender squinted through the peephole at a toothy smiling mouth. Bender unlocked the door. It was the captain; he wasn't smiling, he was grimacing.

"I'll get right to the point. You are a liability on my ship. If this was a different era, I'd throw you overboard."

"I take full responsibility for this."

"So what? That doesn't mean shit."

"How about an apology? I'll do it at the Seder, just before they hide the matzoh."

"Wouldn't help."

"Wouldn't hurt."

"You'd fuck it up."

"If this was a Yom Kippur cruise, I'd be forgiven."

"I'm not Jewish but I believe the deal is that God forgives you, passengers don't."

"What is it I did, exactly?"

"People are saying you're a Holocaust denier."

"What?"

"You said Israel should be wiped off the map, the Jews driven into the sea. There are people looking for you. Big guys with beards and skullcaps."

"This is insane. I'm the guy who wrote *What Would Sandy Do?* It's the number one Jewish movie."

"I saw it. Loved it. I still want you off my ship."

Bender looked out the window. The sun was setting over the Caribbean. "Like in a lifeboat?"

"I'll put you ashore in Labadee. We're close enough."

"I never heard of it."

"It's in Haiti."

"Can I get a plane from there?"

"There are no planes. Royal Caribbean leases it as a cruise destination. You'll leave tonight while everyone's busy at the Seder. Try to get on one of their ships, they go to Miami."

"If I can't?"

"Climb the fence, make your way to Port-au-Prince. Don't worry, they only shoot people climbing in."

o o o

As the *Sea Bream*'s motor launch headed for the beach, Bender saw his life as a series of scenes borrowed from movies or books. Bender as Charles Laughton about to be deposited on Pitcairn Island in *Mutiny on the Bounty*. The dense wall of the distant palm trees was the Amazon jungle, Bender was Tony Last in *A Handful of Dust,* reading Charles Dickens to a mad chief. In his own story, he was a writer found adrift in a lifeboat, blind, half-mad. Taken to the infirmary a beautiful doctor saves his life. His sight returns, his savior is Ellen, who left Hollywood, went to medical school, and became the ship's doctor. They remarry, live happily ever after. It was cheap crap, he knew, and dismissed it all as the launch scraped to a stop on a sand bar. Bender hoisted his suitcase, wrapped his sneakers around his neck, stepped into the Caribbean and waded to the beach. A path led to a clearing where there were swimming pools, water slides, deserted kiosks advertising native art, woodcarvings, food stalls with hand-painted menus for jerk chicken, and a souvenir shop. It was a Haitian Potemkin Village with a water park. Everything was shuttered. A tall Haitian man in a khaki uniform raised his flashlight into Bender's face.

"*Que faites-vous ici?*"

"*Je suis perdu. Parlez-vous Anglais?*"

"Yes. I speak English. How did you get here?"

"I was put ashore. They told me to catch the next ship to Miami."

"It sailed last night. *Oasis of the Seas.* Passover Cruise. I'll help you climb the fence."

Louise wanted to pick him up at the airport, but it would conflict with her 2:40 with Dr. Garcia. Bender took a taxi home, then met her at the Coffee Bean. He told her about the enthusiastic reaction to *What Would Sandy Do?* and how pleasantly surprised he was that *The Dog of Louisiana* held up so well.

"I had fascinating conversations with Arnold Didowitz, Rich Mowbray, even Lawrence Meyers, a real mensch.

Who knew? I went to both Seders and found them surprisingly moving, although it might have been the inspirational singing of the cantors." He told Louise he was looking forward to next week's appointment with Dr. Grotstein because he had done a lot of work.

"Speaking of cruises, didn't Jung say the ego is the cork bobbing on the ocean seeking individuation?" It was one of Bender's favorite metaphors even though he had no idea what it meant.

BEVERLY GLEN

Dear Big John Hayden,

Mr. Hayden, do you remember a night at Dan Tana's? We were a table of admirers, Paul, Mimi, Anthony; an artist, a novelist, a *New Yorker* writer, and me, Bender. You joined us for drinks, then kindly invited us to your suite at The Century Plaza Hotel where, as you put it, we could "talk, smoke and be merry." At the end of the evening, you told me about your appearance before The House Un-American Activities Committee where you gave up the names of friends, colleagues, "I ruined the lives and careers of some good people." You were remorseful, overwhelmed with self-loathing and guilt. I was sympathetic, but I never told you why. It would have required my own confession of betrayal. I was not as honest as you. It has bothered me ever since. May I tell you now?

The first memory is easy, Mr. Hayden. An obese Mediterranean lime tree in Beverly Glen, useless fruit rotting on the ground in front of our house. Two dogs yapping elatedly as I get out of the car. My wife Ellen is sitting on the steps barefoot, wearing jeans and a Grateful Dead t-shirt. She stands, embraces me, the dogs dance around us, we shoo them away, embrace again.

"Terri Winnick's inside. She might be staying with us for a few days. Come say hello. I'll explain later."

The truth of the matter, probably the irony of it, is I had no sense of the consequences of this offer of hospitality. I knew Terri was involved in the Vietnam anti-war movement with Ellen, and likely a member of the same Weather Underground cell, but I didn't know she was a fugitive. I was just a fellow traveler in the war resistance, it had my sympathy, I gave money, wrote fliers and letters, and dreamed of killing Henry Kissinger. I went to demonstrations and marched but avoided arrest. There was one act in the service of the movement that I will tell you about, but if it weren't for court transcripts, taped phone calls, photographs taken by FBI agents, provocateurs, other freelance vermin, my own part in it would be forgotten, I'd have been merely a blip.

The house in Beverly Glen had small windows; unmanageable Southern California vegetation blocked most of the light. I heard Terri before I saw her. It didn't matter. Her voice was the reminder, traces of Long Island with a stop in Madison, Wisconsin.

"Hello, Bender. I hope letting me stay here isn't a big inconvenience."

"Not at all."

In my life, Mr. Hayden, I hid an alternate set of books for an off-Broadway theatre, the love letters of a cousin carrying on an affair, and a phantasmagoric acid flasher's will, "Not to be opened in the event of my death." But I had never hidden a member of a Weather Underground cell. The problem with the house in Beverly Glen was that there wasn't any place to hide, no attic, basement, or crawl space. Anne Frank would have lasted ten minutes. In bed, Ellen said Terri was avoiding a subpoena to testify before a Federal grand jury investigating her cell's activities.

"What are they investigating?"

She moved her mouth close to my ear. "Dynamite."

The days passed. I went to my writing job at CBS, Ellen to her classes at UCLA law school. Terri read, watched soaps, her boyfriend Brad dropped by, occasionally he stayed overnight, leaving early the next morning.

"How long is she going to be here? It's been a week."

"Until Nick says he's ready to turn her in."

Nick Salter, Terri's lawyer; dark brown hair grown long for the left, but not too long, as he needed to move among the proletariat. In profile he was fit for a Soviet poster, hammer and sickle flag furled behind him, Lenin and Ho Chi Minh looking down from the sky at this son of the San Fernando Valley. Nick had read all of Marx by the time he finished high school, organized study groups, believed in dialectic, the inevitability of history, and the eventual triumph of the working class. He was with Tom when they wrote the Port Huron Statement, in Chicago with the 7, on the steps of Sproul Hall in Berkeley with Mario, in Tupelo with Stokely, and now in Venice with Terri, Brad, and Ellen as they fought the grinding obscenity of the Vietnam War. He was married to Marcie Salter. I'll get to her later, Mr. Hayden.

"Ellen, what happens when your parents visit?"

"I don't know. We can't throw her out."

I had a solution. My friend Alan Cooper had given me the keys to his house in the Hollywood Hills while he was in Mexico directing a television movie. "For emergencies," he said. "I would ask you to water the plants, but I know you won't."

The next day I left CBS early, stopped at a supermarket, bought frozen food, canned goods, crackers, and cheeses. I drove back to our house in Beverly Glen. I told Terri I had found a better, more secure "safe house" for her. She liked the term; she had read le Carré. "But here's the deal," I said. "You don't answer the phone, or make calls, you stay inside, you don't tell anyone where you are. Not Nick, Brad, not even Ellen. Okay?"

"Okay."

I made my trips to the house at night, doubling back and forth on the narrow streets above Sunset Boulevard, making sure no one was following me. I parked a block away, slipped into the house, emptied a shopping bag of vegetables and brown rice. I could see that Terri was starting to come apart. She confessed that Nick had been involved in the cell's activities; she was worried that he might be more interested in covering his own activities than helping her. That night Ellen and I met with Nick at Jack's on Lincoln Boulevard.

Ellen said, "You're putting everybody at risk, mostly us, if you don't do something, we're going to bring Terri to your house. You can hide her."

Two days later there was a message from Nick asking me to leave Terri within walking distance of the Federal Building in Westwood. She went into the grand jury, answered all their questions. On the lunch break she took a taxi to LAX, boarded a plane to Vancouver – heads must have rolled for not confiscating her passport – and flew to Tel Aviv. Upon landing she invoked the right of return. Terri Winnick became an Israeli citizen, un-extraditable. Our subpoenas came a year later. Two FBI agents arrived. They asked Ellen if I was home, she told them that I was at NBC. They left subpoenas for both of us.

"I work at CBS," I said.

"I know."

"If they go to NBC and I'm not there…"

"It's not you they want, it's Terri. Jesus."

"That's easy. She's in Israel. I don't have the address of her kibbutz, but I can get it."

"What does the subpoena say?"

"We have to appear at a Federal grand jury in El Paso next month."

"What now?"

"We call Dennis."

Our friend Dennis Roberts, Mr. Hayden, a lawyer in Oakland.

"Here's how it works," Dennis said. "The US Attorney will ask you questions about Terri, why you hid her, demand any information you have that might lead to her or the people who helped her."

"Like Nick?"

"Yes. And yourselves"

"What about my Fifth Amendment right to remain silent, not incriminate myself. What happened to that?"

"It disappeared with the Organized Crime Control Act of 1970, which allowed for the conferring of 'use immunity' to supplant a witness's Fifth Amendment right," Ellen said.

"English. I didn't go to law school like you."

"In a grand jury the judge can be asked to give you 'use immunity,' which means anything you testify to can't be used against you. Use, get it? But they can ask you about other people. For example, if you are asked if you robbed a bank on July 1st and you admit you did, they can't charge you with bank robbery, but if they ask you if Joe Smith was your accomplice you have to tell them."

"That'd be ratting out someone. What if I refuse?" I asked.

"You will be held in contempt of court, taken to jail until you agree to talk or stay in jail until the term of the grand jury ends."

"How long is the term?"

"Eighteen months."

"I can't go to jail for eighteen months. It's pilot season."

I reviewed my crime. A year ago, we hid Terri in our house. The FBI knew that because her boyfriend, Brad Schiffman, who visited her, ate dinner with us, slept with Terri, was an FBI informant. Brad, if that was his real name, claimed to be a disillusioned Vietnam veteran who ended up in Venice where he met Terri, worked his way into the anti-war movement, then her cell. Brad was a good-looking guy whose easy manner and charm went sour after a few drinks. The story, as it went, or was revealed later, was that he got into bar fights. The last one in Palmdale went badly, his victim was an off-duty Hemet cop. Prison was a certainty until the FBI offered him a job informing on his friends in Venice. Brad told me he had written a screenplay; I offered to read it. He handed me a draft of a horror film. I gave him some notes for a rewrite, offered to send it to my agent, but never saw the next draft.

Dennis said we could claim Terri stayed in our house because she needed a break from her Venice roommate. The house was too small, so I found another place for her to stay. My friend Alan returned from his Mexico location surprised to find that his plants were thriving, but he had no idea that it was a fugitive from a grand jury, not me, who had watered them.

o   o   o

At the Federal Courthouse we were given a small office near the Grand Jury courtroom. Extra chairs on risers were provided for the twenty-three citizens of El Paso, all white, mostly retired, who could afford to spend their days listening to government prosecutors interrogate enemies of the state then decide if there was sufficient evidence to indict them. They invariably did. Ellen was called first. Dennis and I waited, twenty minutes later she returned.

"There are two prosecutor. Susan Shea, she's young, looks just out of law school. The other is Gregory Howden. He's in charge, she's asking the boilerplate questions. Name, birthdate, occupation."

"It's all stuff they already know," Dennis said.

"She asked me my name, I refused to answer, told her I wanted to consult with my attorney."

"And?"

"They said I wasn't allowed to leave the room. I knew that wasn't true. I just walked out."

"Do you know what to do now?" Dennis asked.

"Yes. I return, ask them to repeat the question. Then I give them my name."

"Then they will ask you your address, you refuse to answer, you walk out to consult with your attorney. You will do that with all the questions."

Over the next hour the scenario repeated until Shea had all the relevant facts about Ellen. The it was Howden's turn to question her. "Was Terri Winnick a guest in your house?"

Ellen refused to answer. Howden's unanswered questions got more specific, it was clear he knew a lot about Terri, Ellen, Nick, and me. He had dates, places, names, subjects of our conversations, were given to him by Brad. Ellen refused to answer any questions, walked out after each one, returned, repeated "on advice of counsel and my Fifth Amendment right against self-incrimination" and refused to answer the question. At three o'clock Ellen was temporarily excused. It was my turn. I read the same statement, refused to answer questions until it was clear I was also a waste of time. Howden ended the session by announcing that the government would be sending a motion to the District Judge asking that we be granted immunity from prosecution since our forthcoming testimony "was necessary and in the public interest." I was also temporarily excused.

"Let's take a walk," Dennis said. We left the courthouse, found a park. "So far, they don't have shit. They're looking for something to hang Nick with. They don't like him. He defends people they consider enemies, so he's one. Maybe you know something about him they can use, but you don't have it. They're mostly pissed that Terri disappeared for a few days. So we'll make them give you immunity, you'll tell them, and we'll go home."

"It means we will have testified," Ellen said.

"To what? That you hid Terri?" Dennis said. "We'll claim some ancient law of hospitality. The government won't put you in jail for that."

"It's not the government I'm worried about," Ellen said.

"Bender, were there any other conversations you had with Nick about Terri?"

I remembered a stroll on Venice Beach with Brad and Nick, barefoot, our shoes neatly stacked under a deserted lifeguard tower.

"You're a writer, Bender," Nick said. "We need a story to cover a set of events that could have otherwise serious consequences for our friends."

"Can you do that?" Brad asked.

"Maybe. Probably."

"People – you don't need to know who – bought dynamite in El Paso; it was driven to Los Angeles in a car where it ended up in a garbage can against the door of a Bank of America building in Burbank. It didn't go off. But it was Terri's car. Can we find a way to account for her car being in El Paso? But without Terri."

That was an easy one. I imagined myself in a meeting with Levinson and Link, pitching the plot of a *Columbo* episode. "What if Terri loaned the car to someone who left it unlocked, and it was stolen, driven to El Paso. The friend was afraid to admit to Terri that it was missing, hoping that it would be abandoned and found by the cops. Turned out it was in L.A."

"Interesting. It might be possible to produce a person who could testify to having borrowed and then lost the car."

"You'll kill two birds with one stone. One, it's a reason for the car's presence in El Paso, stolen, then possibly used to transport dynamite, and two, Terri's innocence."

"You really did that?" Dennis said.

"Jesus, Bender, you're a fucking idiot," Ellen said.

"What did I do?"

"If you admit to the conversation on the beach where you created an alibi for Terri, Nick is looking at certain disbarment, maybe jail."

"And me?"

"Nothing. You have immunity, remember. But not from perjury."

"So I either tell the truth about the conversation, walk, or lie and save Nick's ass, jeopardizing mine."

"But if they don't know about your conversations, we have a shot to get you out of here."

"What do we have to do?" Ellen asked.

"I go to Howden, find out exactly what he wants to know. If we don't care what he wants us to give him, you tell him, then go home."

"Or refuse to talk."

"The Grand Jury sits for eighteen months. You want to sit in jail that long?"

"No."

"Bender?"

"No. Not for this."

"Okay, let's go."

Dennis went off to call Howden. Ellen said, "Bender, why did you do this?"

"I thought I could be useful."

o   o   o

The District Judge had his considered opinion ready:

"IT IS ORDERED that no testimony shall be used against David and Ellen Bender in any criminal case, except that they shall not be exempted by this order from prosecution for perjury or giving a false statement."

We waited in the little office while Dennis met with Howden. Ellen started biting her nails. Dennis came in. "He only wants to know where you hid Terri. We can be out of here in an hour."

That was it. Sing birds, sing, sing freely knowing you are immune from prosecution. Ellen answered Howden's questions, for the most part truthfully. When did Terri come to our house, why did she come, she knew nothing about dynamite, she did not know where Terri went, or have advance knowledge that Terri planned to flee to Israel? She got through her testimony in twenty minutes and was dismissed.

It was my turn. Dennis coached me to answer reluctantly, "Make it like a confession obtained under duress. You are admitting that you placed a known fugitive in his home without his permission. Make it difficult, be contrite, ashamed."

After I told Howden, he walked back to his table, shuffled some papers, looked up at me; was he measuring my neck size for the noose to hang me when I would be forced to answer his next round of questions, the ones that could put me in jail for perjury.

"Did you ever have any conversations with Nicholas Salter regarding the activities of Terri Winnick?"

"No," I lied.

"Any conversations with Brad Schiffman regarding the activities of Terri Winnick?"

"No," I lied.

"Did you have any conversations with Nicolas Salter or Brad Schiffman regarding the activities of Terri Winnick?"

"No," I lied again.

Howden turned to the jury foreman, "That was my last question. Mr. Bender is excused."

Had Brad forgotten our walk on Venice beach? There was a more charitable explanation: Brad was an amateur forced into the role of informer. I was a friend who encouraged him to write. He saw no reason to burn me.

o   o   o

Our taxi took us home to Beverly Glen, we collected the dogs from our next-door neighbors, a UCLA mathematician, his wife Gabrielle, a French Canadian committed to Quebec separatism who chose to call herself *une nègre blanche.*

"What are you guys doing home?"

A good question. We were supposed to be in jail, in contempt of court for refusing to cooperate with the grand jury. People like Gabrielle were planning to organize defense committees, support groups, feed our dogs, bring us bran muffins on visiting days. Instead, we came home and spoiled everything. Gabrielle knew there was only one reason we were not in jail; we had testified.

"Well?"

Well, what? Did she expect us to tell her how I saved Nick with my perjury? There was no way we explain why we were home, or how we got here, except to say, "I'm sorry, we can't discuss it."

"You can't trust us?"

Trust you? We are out of the trusting business, *Mme. Nègre Blanche.*

"We will be pariahs now," Ellen said, when we were in bed. "The word will get out; people will know we testified. I'm through in this town."

I called Dennis.

"Here's the solution. You meet with Nick, tell him what you testified to without going into details. He'll be eternally grateful. Next, you both do a lot of socializing with Nick and Marcie. Go to restaurants, parties, be seen, make it look like you are still tight so that whatever you did in El Paso was okay with them."

We went to movies at The Fox Theater on Lincoln, a Panther fundraiser at the Ash Grove, a potluck at a Mar

Vista squat, a Malibu cocktail party for the Venice Free Clinic. Movement people got the message: no matter what happened at the grand jury in El Paso, if the Benders and the Salters were friends then everything was cool.

Until the day Marcie Salter summoned Nick into her weaving room, lowered her cup of green tea and announced that she no longer wanted to have anything to do with the Benders.

Nick said, "Yes, dear."

From then on if anyone asked, "How are the Benders?" Marcie replied, "We don't really hang with them anymore."

"Oh, how come? I thought you guys were close."

"I can't discuss it, but we weren't happy with their experience in El Paso."

It only took a few of those exchanges to send our reputations into snitch swamp. For me, it didn't matter. None of the people who employed me, or wanted to hire me, cared. Ellen passed the bar exam but none of the left-wing law firms in Los Angeles would hire her. She ended up working for Marcus Wolfe, a flamboyant criminal lawyer who drove a Rolls-Royce to Superior Court on West Temple where he dealt out drug dealers, gang leaders, and other felons. Ellen specialized in sex workers. "I'd rather defend honest women prostitutes than the male ones you work for at CBS."

There was one other victim, Mr. Hayden: Alan Cooper, my friend who unknowingly lent his house to hide Terri from the FBI. When Special Agent Shaw dropped by for a follow-up chat, Alan didn't know that you never talk to the FBI without your lawyer, and you never let them in your house. Once inside, Special Agent Shaw spotted the ashtray from the Santa Isabel Hotel in Havana. He easily got Alan to admit to a harmless weekend trip to Havana via Mexico City. But visiting Cuba, spending US dollars, and lying about it on his return made him in violation of the Cuban Assets Control Regulations under the Trading with the Enemy Act. The penalties ranged up to ten years in prison and/or $250,000 in fines. The FBI leaked this to an executive at Paramount Pictures. Fearing a loss of cooperation from the Defense Department, Paramount dropped him from his next film, a big-budget war movie that needed their cooperation. Alan spent his savings on a lawyer who negotiated a fifty thousand dollar fine. His William Morris agent fired him. Unemployable, Cooper returned to Minneapolis where he found refuge in alcohol and froze to death in a snowbank on Hiawatha Avenue.

I hear Terri teaches art in Tel Aviv; the Salters moved to Maui. Ellen and I survived, minor casualties of that war, fully limbed, senses intact, un-addicted. We were merely left with guilt, a busted marriage, and some shame. Like you, Big John. The next time I'm in Paris I'll look for your barge near the Pont Alexandre, the one with the green roof.

Yours,
Bender

VENICE

"Is my life imitating a sitcom or is a sitcom imitating my life?" Bender asked Steve as they shared a joint while they watched the Lakers lose to San Antonio. "What I am saying, is that I feel like I lived through a sitcom story minus the stuff you can't do at eight o'clock."

"Like sex?"

"Death." Bender took another hit and coughed. "Okay, also sex."

That was the trouble with weed, Bender thought. It makes you stupid.

"So, tell me the story," Steve said.

o   o   o

It began at Versailles, a Cuban restaurant on Venice Boulevard, where Juliet asked Bender for a favor.

"What's the favor?"

"You live in the Uni High district, right?"

"I believe I do."

"Rachel is at Venice, she hates it."

Bender took another bite of *Lechon Asado*, leaned back, relieved. He had assumed the favor was about rent, a screenplay, or adopt a dog Juliet had just rescued.

"I'll do it," Bender said.

"You didn't hear the favor yet."

"I know what it is. You want Rachel to use my address, so she can say she lives in my house and transfer to Uni High. Of course, she can."

"You are so sweet." Juliet squeezed his hand in a steel grip. "Shall we go?"

Bender was attracted to Juliet but never sure why. A Feldenkrais therapist, super intelligent, she owned a sarcastic wit but was also saddled with a volatile and unpredictable temper. She was unusually high strung for a teacher of the gentle art of awareness through movement. What did Bender find so attractive about this woman who inhabited the edge of displeasure?

"Could it be," Bender asked Dr. Grotstein, "a desire to satisfy Ellen with Juliet as a stand-in? If I achieve perfection in Juliet's eyes, do I atone for failing in Ellen's?"

Dr. Grotstein replied, "You are aware, of course, that Juliet is not your former wife. Usually, it is not a good idea to try to resolve problems with surrogates."

"Ellen never used the words, but I felt it coming from her, unspoken, just like my teachers from kindergarten to college. Bender, you can do better."

"I think you perceive Juliet as a test for you, but it might be wiser for you to affirm your own self-worth than search for it in others."

"But, if I please her, I will have done better, and she will return."

"Perhaps. But her approval will be temporary, there will be an endless succession of challenging women for you not to satisfy."

"Hmm."

"On the other hand, don't let me stop you. My Jaguar needs new tires."

o   o   o

The next day Juliet arrived at Bender's house with a gift. "Isn't she cute?"

"I don't want a dog," he said.

"Why not?"

"I just got rid of one, a boxer. My life improved by twenty per cent."

"How can you quantify that?" Juliet asked.

"I had to take him to the studio, otherwise he shredded my books, He had a weak bladder, so I had to leave meetings to take him out to pee. Walk him when I got home, which made me late for yoga. He ripped holes in screen doors when the raccoons showed up, howled at the TV, chewed my shoes, and worst of all, he only barked at Black people. I once spent a whole session with Dr. Grotstein discussing the dog. After-wards, I realized that I had just spent three hundred dollars talking about an animal. I was crazy, not the dog."

"Don't worry, this one is sweet," Juliet said.

"No dogs."

"Okay. I'll let you know when you need to come to Uni High."

"For what?"

"When Rachel registers. You need to sign some papers. It's no big deal."

o   o   o

"Everything I told you has the structure of a sitcom episode. The hero, me, agrees to do a simple favor, it escalates into comedic chaos. It's pure Aristotle. I just gave you a little bit of act one," Bender said to Steve.

"I don't know Aristotle," Steve said. "But if that's your A-story, what's your B-story?"

"How do you know A from B?"

"I own a deli. I feed writers. Tell me the rest."

"Later."

"You up for some tennis?" Steve said.

"No, thanks. I have to read a script."

Bender drove west on Sunset Boulevard to Will Rogers State Beach. It was late Sunday afternoon when the beach population changed. Anglos departed; Latino families arrived. Men carried coolers full of drinks and food across the sand, their kids kicked soccer balls, older brothers watched their sisters duck waves while their mothers laid out food on folding tables.

"Why?" he asked Cecilia, his housekeeper.

"Iglesia, Señor Bender. We work hard all week, party Saturday night, sleep late Sunday, go to church, then the beach."

"I see," he said, enlightened.

"Also, parking is free after four."

Like many Angelenos, Bender carried you-never-know supplies in the trunk of his car: a ten-year-old earthquake-survival kit with a space blanket, first aid pouch, flares, dehydrated Chicken à la King, matches, a Lacoste polo, and a solar-powered radio. For the beach, in a backpack, a towel, rolled grass mat, sunscreen, bathing suit and goggles. Bender pulled into the Will Rogers Beach parking lot, locked his wallet in the glove compartment, moved his seat back and changed into his bathing suit. He left the script on the passenger seat.

Bender trudged along the water's edge until he found a family listening to K-LOVE. He tossed his backpack on the sand, ran as fast as he could into the Pacific and met a wave that knocked him on his ass.

o   o   o

Bender met Juliet and Rachel on the steps in front of Uni High. "I really appreciate you doing this for me, Mr. Bender."

"My pleasure," Bender said.

"I like Venice, but I can take more AP classes at Uni. I want to go to Berkeley."

"And then?"

"Law school."

"If I sue Stephen King for plagiarism, will you take my case?"

Rachel held out her hand. "It's a deal, Mr. Bender."

This girl had none of her mother's edginess, Bender thought. She possessed a gentler soul, slow to anger. Bender wondered if she could be a good lawyer. Rachel stood one step lower than Bender, but they were eye to eye. She was almost six feet tall with sun-bleached hair, blue eyes, the springy legs of a beach volleyball player, her smile revealed a tiny gap between her top front teeth she must have inherited from her father. There were a few adolescent pimples under the bridge of her glasses to heal, and now that she would be attending the high school of her choice, she had a wider smile.

Bender glanced at Juliet, smiling proudly at her daughter; *behold my brilliant, beautiful daughter, a girl now, who will become a woman I won't live to see.*

○   ○   ○

Bender rode a wave back to the beach, plopped down on his mat. The K-Love couple unfolding the picnic table a few yards away waved hello.

The woman said, *"¿Señor, te gusta esta música?"*

"Me encanta," Bender replied.

"Lo haré más fuerte."

"Gracias."

Bender had nothing to offer in return. Well, maybe. He put his fingers to his lips. The man nodded; they walked to the edge of the water. He wore gangster shorts, a white ribbed singlet. Bender dug into his bag, found a joint and a lighter. The man glanced over his shoulder; his kids were busy helping their mother set the table. Bender lit the joint, inhaled, passed it.

"Thanks."

"Sure."

They watched the beginning of a spectacular sunset, leisurely passing the joint back and forth.

"Pretty cool," Bender said.

"You know why? It's all that shit in the air. Smoke, dust, chemicals, gasses blowing around, the light reflects it, boom, we have beauty."

"It's the price we pay."

"You don't find it ironic?"

"I suppose so." They finished the joint; Bender buried the roach in the sand. He was about to mention that sunsets weren't considered beautiful until painters painted them, or poets wrote about them, but then the man's children, a boy and a girl, tugged at their father's shorts.

"Into the water, Papa. Into the water, Papa."

"You have kids?" the man asked as he let himself be pulled backwards.

"A foster daughter," Bender said. "She goes to Uni."

"I'm Gregory."

"Bender."

Gregory scooped up his boy and girl and waded into the Pacific.

Bender watched him show them how to body surf so they would grow up to be true Californians. They disappeared under a wave, then spit out onto the sand, laughing, hardly able to stand up, charged back into the surf.

o   o   o

In the administrative office, Bender waited while a Vice-Principal helped Rachel fill out forms. Bender, remembering his own high school administrators, thought she was too young, too unscarred. Had she leap-frogged from the classroom to her present position like Moses Malone, who went directly from high school to the NBA? She glanced at him through reading glasses attached to a neckband, shook her head of red hair, dislodging the glasses that landed on her chest.

"Mr. Bender, what's your... our... ZIP code?" Rachel asked.

"90210," Bender said.

"Beverly Hills?" The Vice-Principal said.

"Beverly Hills Post Office." The addition of "Post Office" was an address oddity that benefited west side real estate interests and allowed certain neighborhoods, like Bender's, to use the Beverly Hills ZIP code, and add value to homes, but not attend their schools. Bender was once in an automobile accident in Beverly Hills, his car was undrivable, and the senior officer told a patrolman to drive him home.

"But he lives in Post Office."

"You can drop me off at the border," Bender said.

Rachel handed the form to Juliet. "Your turn, Mom."

Juliet signed. "Now you," Juliet said to Bender, "There and there."

Bender signed twice, affirming under the penalty of perjury that Rachel's residence was his house in Benedict Canyon.

"Is Rachel your daughter, Mr. Bender?" the Vice-Principal asked.

"No."

"Do you have a foster-care license?"

"Sorry?"

"A foster-care license. You'll need one."

"Why?"

"Rachel's a minor. If she's living in your house and you are the custodial parent, then you must be a licensed foster parent for her to be enrolled at University High."

Rachel looked at Bender. *Save me, Bender. Save me from Venice High.*

"How do I get a license?"

The Vice-Principal handed him a brochure, 'How to Become a Foster Parent.'

"I'm sorry, I didn't get your name."

She raised her ID badge.

"Ah, Ms. McCarthy. Pleased to meet you," Bender said.

Bender considered the two women, the Feldenkrais Juliet, and the Vice-Principal Ms. McCarthy. Juliet's goodwill was temporary; life with her would be cold snow in a bipolar arctic landscape. Bender, who wrote scenarios for a living, also wrote them about the people he observed; a driver at a stop light prompted him to a quick biography; the man looked worried, he was on his way to his doctor for test results, they would be good, a celebration to follow. A woman at the Gelson's checkout, her daughter in the shopping cart, was going to drop her off for a play date, then go on to her tennis lesson with her instructor, who was also her lover. Bender was usually wrong, remembering the time he cast Julie Epstein his jogging partner as a retired garment manufacturer, who turned out to be an Oscar-winning screenwriter.

Here, in the Uni High office, Bender charged ahead and imagined life with Ms. McCarthy, his own Grace O'Malley, the Irish Catholic warrior who would end his obsession with Ellen. Bender expanded his plot; he read Yeats, Joyce, O'Casey, ate corned beef and cabbage; would Ms. McCarthy find room for Roth, Singer, Bellow, and borscht? He went further; pictured them in bed; her ID badge, reading glasses, and clipboard, like articles of clothing, slowly removed to 'O'Sullivan's March' by the Chieftains. Would Ms. McCarthy hear Bernstein's 'Kaddish' as Bender took off his socks?

In Hebrew school the Rabbi warned Bender and his fellow bar mitzvah students, "Let me tell you about marrying a shiksa. You could be happy for years, have children, think everything is fine, but one day, God forbid, you will find yourself in an argument with your wife, and she will lose her temper." He paused, allowing the twelve-year-old-boys to picture an argument with a wife. "And then, she will call you a lousy Jew." Ignoring the warning, Bender loved and married Ellen, a Methodist. Bender waited for the "lousy Jew" shoe to drop but the nearest she came was in a Second Avenue delicatessen in response to a surly waiter, "Don't Jewish people have old age homes?"

"Mr. Bender? Are you with us?" Ms. McCarthy said.

"Sorry, I was daydreaming. I do it when I'm in a school."

"Some things you never get over," she said.

Did Bender just hear an inflection? An echo of shtetl-speak, syntax reversed, one that might be uttered in the kitchen of a Fairfax floor-through?

"Read this pamphlet, it will tell you about the process. You need to go to a Human Services office, fill out an application, they will give you a temporary license which you will return it to me."

"And in the meantime, Rachel can enroll?"

"Yes, but there is a deadline for getting the permanent license. If you miss it, she'll be asked to leave."

Ms. McCarthy's instructions, politely given, betrayed no skepticism regarding residence issues or the charade she must suspect was being played out in her office. Bender was impressed. The hell with the rabbi. He was ready to make another leap into religious miscegenation.

In the parking lot, Juliet said, "I'm sorry. I didn't know you'd need to get a license."

"It's okay. I can do it tomorrow."

"You're awesome," Rachel said.

"It's nothing, really."

o   o   o

The clerk at Human Services showed Bender how to fill out the foster parent license application. When he finished, she stamped it and stuck her finger in his chest.

"You will make a child very happy. God will bless you."

Bender called Juliet from Langer's, where he had treated himself to a pastrami sandwich for his good deed. "I have the license. I'll drop it off tomorrow."

"I can't thank you enough. Are you sure you don't want a cute puppy?"

"No, thanks, but what about dinner, or a Feldenkrais tonight at my place?"

"I can't. I have plans."

Plans? Plans for what? World domination? Discovering a cure for cancer? Sex with a biker? Bender was no dope. He knew 'plans' was code for a date.

"Okay, what about the weekend? Santa Barbara? Palm Springs?"

"I have the dogs. They need to be fed."

"Maybe Rachel could do it."

"I'd rather not ask her. She's pretty busy."

I just committed perjury to get your daughter into Uni High. You don't want to ask her? Run, Bender, run.

o o o

The next Sunday at Will Rogers, Gregory admitted he wasn't crazy about K-LOVE's playlist. *"Endless corazones heridos, corazones rotos, corazones reparados,* commercials for McDonald's, Worthington Ford in between. But today's Adela's turn, she gets to choose the music."

"You?"

"I'm all over the place. Right now, I'm into Reuben Blades. You?"

"I got locked into jazz when I was a kid. Sometimes I think I want to get out."

"Just go Latin, man. I'll give you some names."

They sat on the last bit of dry sand and watched Gregory's kids playing in the waves. Gregory offered a loaded clay pipe. "My father steered me into CalArts, I majored in character animation, got a job at Disney. I enjoyed it but I wanted to paint so I quit. My work explored Cholo culture, takes on the border, Día de los Muertos, the immigrant experience. I was an instant success. Got a gallery, Corcoran, Hollywood agents were buying my paintings like crazy. Maybe they wanted to show how they were down with La Raza or impress their maids. Then I realized nobody in the community could afford my work. I got really depressed."

"You don't look very depressed."

"Man, I couldn't afford it. It was a bourgeois luxury. Marrying Adela helped."

"Wait a minute. I know you. You're Gregory Romero, right?"

"Yep."

"You used to have a Christmas studio sale."

"Still do."

It came back to Bender; Gregory opened his studio in Highland Park to neighborhood kids; he created his own weekend art school. The week before Christmas he put up their work for sale.

"I throw in some prints of mine but it's really to give my students a way to show off, hopefully sell some of their art."

"I went a few years ago. There was a woman who painted postage stamps with faces of gardeners. I bought them."

"Adela." Gregory turned around, "Honey, this guy collects you."

"Come eat with us," she said.

Bender felt a glow. What a wonderful place is Los Angeles! Will Rogers, who never met a man he didn't like, would be proud of this beach that bore his name. I can drive here, sit at the water's edge, smoke weed with a man who turns out to be a wonderful artist. His wife, also an artist, invites me to share their picnic dinner and I have her art in my house in Benedict Canyon. Does this happen in the Hamptons? Do people drive to the beach in the Hamptons after church? He didn't know, he had never been to the Hamptons. Bender had once rented a summer house on Topanga Beach; a one-story rectangular box on the Pacific Coast Highway that looked like a giant sardine can on stilts. He had a view of the Pacific from his balcony, but the deserted beach was underwater most of the day. At night he thought he was being lulled to sleep by the sound of the breaking waves, but he was hearing the hum of traffic on the Pacific Coast Highway. Awakening to foggy mornings, he had to drive two miles to Malibu to get a *New York Times* and a bagel. Bender broke the lease, moved back to Benedict Canyon, and happily drove to Will Rogers, where he could talk to people.

"Are you painting now?" Bender asked.

"Not sure what to call it. Adela comes from a town near Puerto Escondido. They make clay planters and big vases; I paint them with scenes of village life, in the style of Corinthian Greek pottery. Come to our studio. I'll show them to you."

Adela added, "You can see my new work."

"Can I bring my girlfriend?" Bender said, even though he didn't have one.

o   o   o

Ms. McCarthy looked at the temporary foster care license, nodded, and her glasses fell. "Let me know when you get the permanent one."

Her eyes were bright green; there were tiny freckles on her white cheeks. It was now or never. "I will," Bender said. "By the way, can I call you?"

"What for?" She replaced the glasses, Bender felt a Vice-Principal's stare.

"To tell you when I get my license, maybe we could have a drink."

She hoisted the glasses to her nose.

"To celebrate, I mean," Bender said.

"Just bring in the license."

"How's she doing?" Bender added, trying to sound like a concerned foster parent.

"Who?"

"Rachel."

"You don't know? She's living with you, right?"

"I meant academically."

"Talk to her guidance counselor. Don't call me in the mornings, after four is best. I live in Santa Monica. We could go to Robert's; they make good martinis. And don't forget to make an appointment with the social worker."

o   o   o

He met Juliet at the Rose Cafe. "I have a meeting with a social worker. She is coming to my house."

"So?"

"She's going to interview me and inspect the house to make sure it's a healthy environment for your daughter. It's called a Full Family Assessment"

"So?"

"I live in a one-bedroom house. What am I going to say, she sleeps with me?"

"Calm down. I don't like you when you get excited. What about your office?"

"It's my office. It's where I work."

"We can convert it to her bedroom."

Juliet and Rachel arrived in a borrowed Toyota pick-up loaded with a bed, mattress, blankets, pillows, and suitcases. They lugged it all into Bender's office, covered the bed with Rachel's stuffed dolls. Juliet took down his Mapplethorpe nudes.

"They're kind of gross, don't you think?"

"If they were gross, I wouldn't have them," Bender said.

"I like them, Mom," Rachel said.

"Sorry, honey, they have to go." Juliet also removed his Louise Brooks photo, put up Rachel's Axl Rose. She replaced the *Bande à part* poster with a Madonna, swept everything off Bender's desk including his Writers Guild award, planted Rachel's textbooks, sharpies, colored pencils, erasers, and notebooks in neat piles. Moving to the bathroom, Juliet filled a wicker basket with tampon boxes, her organic soaps, and vegetable shampoos.

"Anything else?"

"I brought her dog."

"No dogs."

The social worker from Human Services checked items on her clipboard as Bender gave her a tour of the house, pointing out Rachel's bedroom, her bathroom, the kitchen and living room. He skipped the hot tub. She accepted his offer of ginger tea.

"You'll be approved. You should get the permanent license in a few weeks."

o o o

Ms. McCarthy was waiting for him at Robert's, a window table with a fine view of the ocean. Her first name was Sandra. They quickly covered the Los Angeles conversation markers: smog, traffic, earthquakes, fires, and agreed they were living in paradise; they put a few personal cards on the table. Bender went first, "I have one failed marriage under my belt. I'm being closely monitored by an eminent Westwood shrink. Neil Navitz is my agent, I had a happy childhood."

"I'm impressed."

"Navitz?"

"The happy childhood. My turn? We're even in the failed marriage department, I'm sorry I don't know who Neil Navitz is, and by the way I hope you don't play golf. I consider it an elitist use of green space."

Bender couldn't believe his luck; he had a story to go with golf. "I had a job in a Century City office that overlooked the L.A. Country Club, the one Victor Mature couldn't get into. When he was told the club excluded actors, he said, 'I'm not an actor and I've got twenty movies to prove it.'"

"That's a good one."

"From my window, I looked out on 250 acres of the most beautiful land in Los Angeles and never counted more than twenty people on it at any time. Shall I order another martini, should we stay for dinner?"

"Yes, to both, please. Do you have a first name?"

"David. But I prefer Bender."

They went quiet, but the silence was comfortable as they peered out the window: the sun setting behind moving cyclists, joggers, and skaters on the bike path; the volleyball courts were deserted, two bodybuilders pumped iron at Muscle Beach, further north, the lights of the Santa Monica Pier came alive. Sandra and Bender turned from the window, each hoping to steal a glance of a profile while the other wasn't looking; but because it happened at the same moment they simply shrugged and smiled with an unspoken suspicion that this might lead to serious love if they didn't fuck it up, so Bender didn't try to imagine her story, he let her tell it.

"Northwestern, I majored in linguistics, but it was too hard, so I switched to education. I got my license, taught English in Tokyo, Milan, and Moscow, came back to L.A., and ended up in administration."

"Do you like it?"

"For now, yes. I get to help kids. Or try to."

"Later?"

"I think I want to write children's books. There's one more thing. I'm coming out of a divorce. My shrink says I'm not ready for a relationship. Are you in a hurry?"

Bender was always in a hurry. He dived into swimming pools, ran into oceans, he never dipped his toe first. He read on the toilet, wrote while he watched TV, listened to news in the shower, did the crossword puzzle at red lights. He was in such a hurry for Sandra that he told her he wasn't in a hurry. They began slowly, meeting for simple and chaste lunches, knees not bumping under the table at Baja Bud's or The Apple Pan counter, graduated to dinners in Culver City and

Koreatown, always splitting the bill. They made a day trip to Ojai in Sandra's white Beetle with the top down, neither of them brought a just-in-case toothbrush. Josh Rosen, who directed Bender's sitcom asked, "How's your social life these days?"

"I'm seeing someone but we're taking it slowly."

"You? Give me a break."

○ ○ ○

Juliet came to Bender's house with her new boyfriend, the owner of the Toyota pick-up, they collected Rachel's toilet articles. "I think we're in the clear," Juliet said.

Bender had gotten used to Rachel's staged bedroom, he liked the idea of an imaginary child, was he ready for a real one? In any event, it made his house seem less lonely while he was not hurrying Ms. McCarthy.

"Maybe we should leave the bed. We might get a drop-in from the social worker. I say leave the bed."

On a hike in Sullivan Canyon, Sandra told him not to use his headset. "Pay attention to nature, Bender, it's talking to you." He removed the ear pods and heard birds sing, twigs crack under his sneakers, a LAPD helicopter buzzing overhead. Ahead of them on the path a gaunt coyote, considering Bender and Sandra food, stared. Bender growled first; the animal slinked off.

Sandra took his arm, "Nice, Bender."

It was two months now. Even though they hadn't been inside their homes, they were almost a couple, so Bender thought it was time to come clean. "I was thinking how we met. You remember Rachel and her mother…"

"Her teachers say she's doing well."

"About her enrolling. I want to tell you..."

"It's okay. Some things you don't want to know."

There it was again: the inflection.

o   o   o

Sandra and Bender took the 10 Freeway to the Romeros' house, a dramatic three-story modernist structure built into the side of a hill in Highland Park between Dodger Stadium and the Los Angeles Police Academy. The first floor was Gregory's studio, the second, Adela's, the third housed a kitchen, living room, the family bedrooms. Gregory's paintings leaned against the walls of his studio, more were stacked on wooden shelves, paint cans with hardened brushes bunched in disarray were strewn on tables; sketches tacked to cork boards, there was a commercial kiln in the corner surrounded by waist high ochre pots waiting to be painted and fired, all of it demonstrating an artist's energy that made Bender feel like a dabbler. He was no stranger to artists' studios, but he had never seen one bursting with creativity like Gregory's. He had read Henry Adams' account of seeing a dynamo at the Chicago Exposition and sobbing when he had no idea how it worked. Bender didn't shed Henry's tears, but standing amid all this artwork made his own seem insignificant.

Gregory's pots were parodies of ancient Greek amphora; instead of Achaean warriors wielding spears, he portrayed Mexican *campesinos* slashing cacti, in place of chariots, there were Nissan trucks.

"The dogs are the same," Ms. McCarthy said. "They still chase rabbits, hunt boar, and scrounge for scraps."

"Exactly," Gregory said.

On the second floor, Adela's studio opposed the anarchy of Gregory's. It mirrored her art; it was ordered, minimal, precise.

"I'm not doing the gardener postage stamps any more," she said.

Adela spread out a large portfolio on her table. Using delicate ink strokes, she had drawn portraits of Latino workers waiting at bus stops: hotel maids, cleaning ladies, nannies, kitchen help, the people who depended on city buses to take them from jobs in Brentwood, Beverly Hills, and Santa Monica to their homes in East L.A., Maywood, and Boyle Heights. Three weary women on a bench clutching their purses, two housepainters sharing a quart of Coca Cola, a man looking at the bus schedule trying to make sense of his route, restaurant workers in white shirts, black pants, baseball jackets over their shoulders, the ones who made Los Angeles run on minimum wages. Adela's drawings were frank, unsentimental, as finely executed as Dürer.

"Can we buy them?" Ms. McCarthy asked.

"Not until after dinner," Adela said.

On the way home, Bender exited the Hollywood Freeway at Cahuenga and drove up to Mulholland Drive. When he came to a spot where they could see the blinking electric carpet of Los Angeles stretching to the ocean, he parked the car.

"It's spectacular even when you're not a tourist," Ms. McCarthy said. They leaned against the warm engine. "If Gregory painted a vase for you, what would you want on it?"

"Me at my portable Royal, my father showing me how to grip the tennis racquet, my mother teaching me piano. What about you?"

"I'd ask Gregory to paint me with Cinderella at Disneyland, on a Bateau Mouche with the Eiffel Tower in the background and…"

Bender forgot he wasn't supposed to be in a hurry, "Would you insist on raising our children Catholic?"

"…and my mother and me at my Bat Mitzvah."

"I beg your pardon?"

"McCarthy is my married name. I didn't tell you? I could change it back to Cohen, but the kids at Uni know me as McCarthy." She shook her head; he felt her reading glasses on his chest as they kissed.

"You know what, Bender? You're the best."

"I could do better," he said.

"Did you hear what I just said? You're the best."

"Really?"

"Really." Sandra replaced her glasses. "I think I'm done not hurrying."

"Rachel is camping in Joshua Tree. We'll have the house to ourselves."

It wasn't a crazy passionate embrace in the doorway like in a movie. They didn't leave a trail of clothes on the way to the bedroom. They went to the kitchen where Bender made tea and gave her a tour of the house. He showed her the hot tub without an invitation to soak.

"I like the way your house is, Bender. You left space."

He knew what she meant.

o   o   o

A few weeks later Rachel graduated from Uni High. Bender offered to ship everything to her dorm at Berkeley, but she drove to Benedict Canyon, picked out a few dresses, took down her posters, said he could keep the rest, including the bed. Bender donated everything to Goodwill, re-hung his Mapplethorpe nudes, his Godard poster, the Louise Brooks, and his share of Adela's bus stop portraits. He left a section of the wall blank for Sandra.

Over morning coffee on the deck, Sandra said, "It's time to meet my parents, Bender. Tomorrow night."

"Do I dress?"

"You have to ask?"

o   o   o

It was a Shabbat dinner at Sandra's parents' house in Glendale. Her mother, Florence, worked at the Central Library and had Sandra's red hair; her father, Antonio towered over Bender. He owned a boxer's face: nose askew, rough ears, puffy eyelids. He was an optometrist. After they shook hands, Antonio held Bender's jaw in one hand, with the other he removed his eyeglasses, made swift delicate bends to the frame, and replaced them.

"Better?"

"Much."

Sandra's older brother, Bobby, came with his husband, Tod; they owned a Foot Locker in Manhattan Beach and invited him to come by for sneakers at a family discount. The Cohens were Sephardic Jews; there was no Yiddish. Bender was greeted with *Buen Shabat*, the blessings for wine and food were also in Ladino. Florence served Moroccan beef soup, chicken with apricots, then brought out her hash pipe with the dessert, a sweet Meskouta orange cake. Bender felt warm and welcome, he could even see himself a member of the family. He was falling, as Neil Navitz might have said, for the package, but in his next session with Dr. Grotstein he said, "I have to be careful that I don't fall in love with her family instead of Sandra."

"You might be entitled to both" replied Dr. Grotstein.

o   o   o

The next Friday, after dinner, Antonio invited Bender to his study. He poured two tiny glasses of cognac. "A question, Mr. Bender."

"Certainly."

"Do you plan to marry my daughter?"

Bender hesitated.

"Well? Yes, or no?"

Bender considered the odds. Antonio was rock, he was paper. But he wouldn't be intimidated.

"No."

"What do you mean by no?"

"By no," Bender said, "I mean yes."

o   o   o

"You still don't have a B story," Steve said.

"Yes, I do. Juliet's boyfriend didn't love her enough when she got sick, so Rachel moved back to Venice to take care of her. She was in her first year of law school at Bolt."

"And?"

"Come with me to Will Rogers, I'm meeting Sandra and the Romeros."

In the car Bender continued, "You remember Vernon Segal? He was a big screenwriter who had a serious crush on Juliet, they dated for a while, he even proposed, but she turned him down. They had mutual friends, so they kept running into each other at dinner parties. One night, she told him about her cancer. Vernon said, 'I know what you should do. Marry me.' The gossip said Vernon married Juliet to claim an inheritance but that was just an old movie plot. They married because Vernon's Writers Guild Health Plan would cover Juliet's doctors, hospital, chemo, a nutritionist, the expenses of staying alive with stage-four breast cancer. Vernon was a mensch. The Writers Guild didn't need to know it wasn't romantic love."

"That is a B-story. Maybe an A."

"There's more. Everybody figured a small civil ceremony in the Santa Monica courthouse, but Vernon got carried away and arranged a blowout wedding at the Hotel Bel-Air. I went with Sandra. We drank champagne on the little bridge, fed crackers to the swans, ate lobster from the seafood mountain, and I consumed a thousand mini-smoked salmon pizzas personally made by Wolfgang Puck. Bobby Davies, twenty years sober from Robertson AA, married them in a faux Buddhist ceremony. Juliet wore a vintage Holly Harp, carried a matching white Pekinese that bit Vernon when he kissed her. Rachel told me the reason she wanted to go to Uni High wasn't because of AP classes at Venice, she had a boyfriend in Brentwood. I proposed to Sandra, and she said yes. We're here."

Bender drove into the parking lot. On the beach Sandra and the Romeros were setting the picnic table.

"Finish the story," Steve said.

"After everyone went home, Vernon told Juliet he booked a suite so they could consummate the marriage. Juliet told him he was out of his mind and took a taxi back to Venice. She died three months later."

"Oh, man, that's not a sitcom. I don't even know what it is," Steve said.

Maybe it's about lies, Bender thought. He lied so Rachel could go to Uni High, Vernon lied to the Writers Guild so he could get insurance for Juliet, the beautiful sunset at Will Rogers Beach was just smog and chemicals.

Bender didn't tell Steve that at last week's Academy screening he had seen Ellen enter with a man. They were holding hands. Bender watched them settle into their seats, a few rows in front of him. The man put his arm around Ellen, she tilted her head against his shoulder, and she looked like she knew why he loved her. Bender waited for Jealousy and Despair to join him. At the same moment, Sandra put her head on his shoulder and squeezed his hand. Bender figured Messrs. J&D were busy elsewhere.

Bender and Steve trudged across the sand, and as often happens to writers who write comedy, an old joke came to Bender, one that Will Rogers might have told while he twirled his lasso.

"There were these two farmer brothers, Marcus and Clem. One day Clem bursts in waving a newspaper. "Lookee here, Marcus, there's a circus coming to town, and they got an elephant!" Since it was market day, the brothers loaded their wagon with eggs, fruits, and vegetables and headed for town. Just as they arrived the circus parade started. Right up front was the elephant. The horses spooked, they bucked and kicked, overturned the wagon, and sent the whole load into the muddy street. There was broken eggs and produce strewn in every direction. Marcus screamed, "We're ruined! We're ruined!"

"I don't give a damn," Clem said, "I have seen the elephant."

Bender heard the slap of the Pacific waves; the silence in between filled with children laughing. A beach volleyball landed at his feet. He picked it up and tossed it back to the players.

Bender didn't care why Ellen had left him, he was glad he had come to Hollywood, the hell with Puerto Vallarta. He had played tennis with Abbie Hoffman, smoked weed with Sterling Hayden, jogged with Julie Epstein, was a character in a Mimi Betz novel, had told a drug kingpin (albeit generic) he was a motherfucker, ate oysters in Cannes, armed himself against a jealous rival, deducted Paris, and was living happily ever after with Sandra. They had a son on the way who would be called Fred.

He had seen the elephant.

"Bender, hurry," Sandra said, "Food's getting cold."

ACKNOWLEDGEMENTS

It has been my good fortune to have friends and family who read early versions of *Bender's L.A.*, those who praised it and those who told me how to make it better. What more could a writer want?

I am therefore indebted to Lili Anolik, Eve Babitz, John Baxter, Jessica Anya Blau, Ernest Chambers, Fred Elias, Susan Elias, Niki Fink, Howard Franklin, David Freeman, Arnold Kogen, Sheila Malovany, Steve Martin, Patrick McGilligan, Nicholas Myer, Caroline Michel, Tom Pabst, Petru Popescu, Dennis Roberts, Ruth Rogers, Melvin Scheer and Dale Herd, a magnificent writer who so generously took time from his own work to help me with mine.

My grateful thanks to artist Deborah Blum for the beautiful cover image and to Mike Zikovitz for his elegant book design.

Bringing a book to life is often a difficult and contentious process. Publisher Paul Cronin and his Sticking Place Books made it easy.

I write this on my knees: words will fail me in expressing my gratitude to Bianca Roberts, my wife, and the most useful critic and supporter I could have. Without her, *Bender's L.A.* would merely be an idea.

ABOUT THE AUTHOR

Michael Elias grew up in the Catskill Mountains, a Red Diaper Borscht Belt Baby in a world of blacklisted artists, intellectuals, tummlers, folk singers, boxers, and Jewish gangsters, (some of whom sleep at the bottom of Loch Sheldrake). His childhood heroes were Jerry Lewis, Harry Belafonte, Rocky Marciano, and Abe 'Kid Twist' Reles. Educated in the classics at St. John's College, Elias took his knowledge of ancient Greek and mathematics to New York, trained at the Actors Studio and acted in The Living Theatre, La MaMa, and the Judson Poets Theatre. From there he dove into stand-up comedy, playing coffee shops, night clubs and *The Tonight Show*. Fired from Ed Sullivan, he abandoned the act, moved to Hollywood where he wrote sitcoms, variety shows, screenplays, and participated in the anti-Vietnam War movement, earning a subpoena to a Nixon grand jury. Elias continues to write novels and screenplays in Los Angeles, where he lives with his wife Bianca Roberts and their dachshund Mabel.

www.ingramcontent.com/pod-product-compliance
Lightning Source LLC
Chambersburg PA
CBHW021348150726
47989CB00005B/2156

9 798899 760686